shatter the stillness. "It's almost a palpable thing, velvety soft like a cushion against the rough edges of the world."

Mitch kissed the top of her head. "Do you know what gets to me around here?"

Tiffany looked up at him and shook her head.

His smile was heart-tuggingly tender. "You." Touching his lips to each of her eyelids, he said, "You get to me, Tiffany Greer, whether you mean to or not."

"Mitch," she whispered. "Oh, Mitch . . ." She couldn't think of another thing to say, but it didn't matter. His mouth was covering hers, and she lay across his lap, her arms around his neck and her fingers furrowing through the tousled silk of his hair.

"Tiffany, what am I going to do with you? I spend half my time making serious promises to myself that I'll keep my hands off you, and the other half breaking those promises."

Her lips toyed with his, her tongue coaxed his lips apart. "Break those promises, Mitch. Just for a little while. No strings."

He surrendered to her entreaties, but he knew she was wrong. There were strings binding them together, and there had been from the beginning. . . .

WHAT ARE *LOVESWEPT* ROMANCES?

They are stories of true romance and touching emotion. We believe those two very important ingredients are constants in our highly sensual and very believable stories in the LOVESWEPT line. Our goal is to give you, the reader, stories of consistently high quality that may sometimes make you laugh, sometimes make you cry, but are always fresh and creative and contain many delightful surprises within their pages.

Most romance fans read an enormous number of books. Those they truly love, they keep. Others may be traded with friends and soon forgotten. We hope that each LOVESWEPT romance will be a treasure—a "keeper." We will always try to publish

LOVE STORIES YOU'LL NEVER FORGET
BY AUTHORS YOU'LL ALWAYS REMEMBER

The Editors

Loveswept® 633

STORMY WEATHER

GAIL DOUGLAS

BANTAM BOOKS
NEW YORK · TORONTO · LONDON · SYDNEY · AUCKLAND

STORMY WEATHER

A Bantam Book / August 1993

To Al, for weathering so many storms with us.

ONE

Tiffany Greer stared in wide-eyed shock at the ground far below. All those farewell jokes by her friends and co-workers didn't seem so funny at the moment.

"Is something wrong?" the elderly woman sitting next to her asked.

Tiffany glanced up.

"You gasped," the woman explained, smiling at Tiffany's quizzical expression. "At least, I assume it was a gasp. You looked out the window, and a little squeak came out of you."

Tiffany chewed on her lower lip for a moment, then simply couldn't contain herself. "Mrs. Holt, everything's white down there," she said in a confidential whisper, as if afraid of setting off a panic. "I wondered if it was a bank of clouds, but I can see tiny little headlights. I think the ground is covered with snow. A *lot* of snow."

Mrs. Holt laughed, yet managed to look sympathetic. "Hawaii seems very far away right now, doesn't it?"

Tiffany nodded. "A world away. I was born and brought up in Honolulu. I only left the South Pacific once, and that was for a Mexican vacation. I've never seen snow, except in movies or on postcards, or in one of those tiny glass-bubble igloos you turn upside down."

"Really? You weren't in Hawaii on a holiday? Good heavens, dear, why would someone who lives in paradise *choose* to come to a place like Winnipeg? And in January!"

"It wasn't by choice," Tiffany replied, letting out a long, pent-up sigh. "I was sent. I work for a health food conglomerate that's based in Hawaii but is expanding its horizons. I'm here to check out a Winnipeg firm for a possible share-purchase. If there's a deal, I might have to stay to help with the changeover." She grinned weakly. "I could be here for quite a while."

"Didn't you have any idea what you were getting into when you accepted this assignment?" Mrs. Holt asked, closing her book and sliding it into her handbag.

Tiffany shook her head. "When you're at the bottom of the executive ladder, you don't question orders. You start packing. I did a little bit of research, of course."

"Excellent," Mrs. Holt said, like an approving but amused schoolteacher. "Did you learn what to expect of the climate?"

"I . . . er . . . quit reading when I got to that part," Tiffany said. "Sometimes it's better not to know too much. I'll just have to adapt, I guess. And after all, people do live there. *You* live there. How cold can it be?"

Mrs. Holt opened her mouth to answer, hesitated, and finally reached out to pat Tiffany's hand. "You're probably right, my dear. Sometimes it's better not to know."

Mitch Canfield pulled off his fleece-lined gloves and unzipped his down-filled jacket as he raced into the Winnipeg airport terminal, glancing around the main floor in the hope of spotting the person he was supposed to meet. When he didn't see anyone who filled the bill, he stopped at the nearest Arrivals monitor to find out whether the flight had landed.

Raking his fingers through his dark hair, Mitch scanned the list and swore softly. The plane had been right on time, and he was fifteen minutes late.

He marched to the baggage area. The revolving carousel was empty, and the only remaining passengers, two oriental men in business suits, were engaged in an animated conversation with a long-suffering baggage handler who was trying to get them to fill out a lost-luggage form.

Deciding to have his passenger paged, Mitch was about to head for the information desk when he turned toward a nearby car rental booth and spied a pair of long, shapely legs encased in utterly impractical patent knee-high boots. His gaze traveled upward over a sunny yellow coat that was pretty but next to useless in Winnipeg's sub-zero weather, then on to a cloud of charmingly tousled black hair.

He smiled as he strode over to the booth. The lady had to be the one he was looking for. She clearly hadn't spent much time in the north. "Are you Tiffany Greer, by any chance?" he asked as he reached her.

She looked up from the map she was studying on the counter, and Mitch's pulse took off like a bobsled in a World Cup race. Her eyes were seafoam green and almond shaped, framed by thick black lashes and gently arched brows. High cheekbones dominated delicate features, and a firm chin tried its best to deny the vulnerability suggested by full, soft, inviting lips.

Realizing that she hadn't confirmed her identity, he tried once more. "Are you Tiffany Greer?" he asked, his voice maddeningly hoarse.

Tiffany nodded but didn't speak. Captivated by warm brown eyes and a smile that ought to have melted all the snow in North America, she found herself dwelling on just one thought: *Too bad he's married*. He was most definitely married. His wife helped him run the family farm and food company. "You're Mr. Canfield?" she finally asked, her eyes fixed on the shallow cleft in his chin.

"Right." He thrust out his hand. "But we're not formal around here. The name's Mitch."

Tiffany's smile was guarded as she accepted the handshake. "It's supposed to be Peter."

"Pete's my brother. He asked me to pick you up and drive you out to the farm. A little problem came up that kept him from coming for you himself."

Mitch, Tiffany repeated silently. Maybe he was single after all. He wasn't wearing a ring, she noticed. She also noticed that he was holding her hand longer than necessary. His grip was firm but gentle, his palm sizzling with electricity that zinged all the way up her arm and dispersed through her body in pinpoints of heat. Even with her eyes downcast, she was acutely conscious of his penetrating gaze. Was he reading her thoughts? Did he know that she was tempted to move closer to him to capture his elusive, crisp scent? That the slight bump just below the bridge of his otherwise perfectly chiseled nose was incredibly intriguing? "How did you pick me out of the crowd?" she asked, drawing on sheer willpower to sound detached.

Mitch blinked. "Are you kidding? In that getup?"

Tiffany snatched back her hand. "No, I'm not kidding." She pasted on a cool smile, deciding she didn't want him to know he'd rattled her. "It's not as if I'm wearing a sarong and have a lei draped around my neck."

A dangerous gleam appeared in his eyes, giving Tiffany the impression that he was picturing her in a sarong and a lei. To her vast annoyance, she wanted him to like the picture.

His eyelids came down for an instant, like a shutter.

He zipped up his jacket, put on his gloves, picked up Tiffany's suitcases, and began walking toward the exit, expecting her to trail along after him without question or hesitation.

At first, she did just that. Then, realizing what she was doing, she swore under her breath. If she was going to have the air of authority she needed on this assignment, she'd better start showing a bit more spunk. It was a little late to stop and demand that Mitch Canfield politely *invite* her to follow him, so she tried another tack. "You haven't answered me," she reminded him. "How did you know who I was?"

"Those duds you're wearing are some island designer's idea of winter clothes, that's how. They're perfect for a lady named 'Tiffany,' but . . ."

"So now there's something wrong with my name as well as my clothes?"

"Nothing at all," Mitch answered, grinning over his shoulder at her. For some reason, he found he couldn't resist teasing Tiffany Greer. He liked the way she lifted that stubborn little chin. "It's a very pretty name," he went on without breaking stride. "Suits you perfectly. So does your outfit. Unfortunately, the minute you step outside you're going to freeze your . . ." He laughed. "Let's just say you won't be comfortable unless the temperature suddenly shoots up to a balmy ten below."

Tiffany stopped dead. "Ten below? Below what?"

"Below zero," he answered matter-of-factly. He

turned to give her a questioning look. "Too cold for you?"

The hint of a challenge in his eyes gave Tiffany pause. Did he *want* her to be horrified? It didn't make sense. The owner of Canfield Farm was looking for a corporate partner. The overtures hadn't been made by Paradise Foods, but by Peter Canfield. Why would his brother try to scare her off by exaggerating the weather conditions? "I suppose it's snowing too?" she said, smiling and feeling rather proud of her show of nonchalance. "A little more snow is just what the place needs, right?"

"It's too cold to snow," Mitch answered cheerfully.

Tiffany's grin faded. "Too cold to snow," she repeated in a monotone. "Just how cold would that be?"

"About thirty below, maybe thirty-two, with a windchill factor of around forty-five." His eyes danced as he added, "But hey, it's a *dry* cold."

There was no question about it, Tiffany thought. He was baiting her. Fine. She simply refused to bite. She stood there studying him, debating whether to ask him outright what his problem was. Had she wandered into macho territory? Had he been expecting a man? Not likely, she realized. He'd picked her out of a crowd, and he'd known her name. So what *was* his problem?

"Can we get this show on the road?" he said with exaggerated patience. "I parked at a meter, and they don't allow much time on those things."

"Why are you rushing me?" Tiffany asked, deciding to make a stand. "Come to think of it, why am I going anywhere with you? How do I know you're Peter Canfield's brother? You could be a . . . a kidnapper!" She felt like a fool as soon as she'd made the outlandish statement. Instead of taking a stand, she'd taken a verbal pratfall.

"Do I look like a kidnapper?" he asked, wishing she weren't so appealing, trying to be feisty and making a mess of it.

Tiffany decided to brazen it through, giving him a once-over. It wasn't much help to her peace of mind that she liked what she saw. His brown hair, fairly short and, she suspected, terminally unruly, was all too touchable. His skin was burnished to a warm, golden tan that softened the harsh lines of his weathered face. Under his thick blue jacket and soft, well-worn denims was an obviously great build, and he not only moved with the easy grace and confidence of a natural athlete, he projected coiled energy even when he was standing still.

The man was dangerously attractive. Tiffany activated an inner defense system that had been fail-safe for her for the past three years. "Actually, you look like a ski bum," she said in as disparaging a tone as she could muster.

His only reaction was another grin. "Good guess. But you're stalling, Sweet Leilani, and we both know it's because you dread going outside, not because you question my identity. I don't blame you, but I'd be grateful if you'd come along like a brave girl so I won't end up with a parking ticket." He started toward the door again. "You'd better wait inside while I get the car. I'll have it nice and cozy for you."

Tiffany shot him a withering look and brushed past him as she marched toward the exit. "I'll go with you. There's no need for you to make things cozy for me, thank you."

Mitch stepped in front of her, blocking her way. "Listen, that vehicle will be like the inside of a freezer until I've had time to run the heater. We don't need bravado from someone who has no idea what she's dealing with."

As he turned and started away, Tiffany felt like throwing something at him, but she reminded herself that as soon as she'd been delivered to the Canfields' farm, she need have nothing more to do with their brother. "What kind of car?" she called after him, then couldn't resist adding, "Or is it a team of huskies?"

He glanced back at her. "It's a Jeep Cherokee. A red one. Don't rush out as soon as you see me pull up, though. Stay where you are. I'll come in and get you."

"Why don't you leave my suitcases instead of carrying them all the way out to the car?"

He turned and winked at her as he pushed through the door. "Consider them hostages. We wouldn't want you to get any ideas about running out on us because the weather's too much for you, would we? Pete and Jackie are looking forward to showing you their operation."

Tiffany opened her mouth, but shut it again as she

realized she would be talking to the thick glass of a closed door. And she was confused. Mitch wasn't trying to scare her off after all.

Whatever his game was, though, her patience with his manner had run out.

By the time the red Jeep pulled up in front of the door, she had rehearsed a satisfying speech that would tell him where to get off if he rubbed her the wrong way one more time. And she would *not* wait inside until he came in to help her to the car, as if she couldn't walk three yards on her own.

As he hopped from the vehicle, Tiffany defiantly stepped outside the terminal to meet him, her head held regally high. But the cold air hit her like a wall of ice as a blast of wind took her breath away, and a slippery patch on the sidewalk finished her off. It was as if a rug had literally been pulled out from under her. Arms flailing, fingers clutching at empty air, she was grudgingly grateful for the strong arms that folded around her. She felt her curves softening, fitting themselves to the contours of a hard frame despite several thick layers of clothing.

"I knew I had a good reason to appreciate a brutal day like this one," Mitch said, the low timbre of his voice resonating with humor and sending odd vibrations through her.

Startled by her body's treachery, Tiffany flattened her palms on Mitch's chest and tried to push herself away. When he didn't let her go, she tipped back her head and glared up at him. "What do you think you're doing?"

"Taking advantage of a golden opportunity," he answered with unabashed honesty. "And keeping you from falling on your pretty keister. Your boots have no tread."

"How do you know?" she snapped.

Mitch laughed and gathered her even closer. "What? That your keister is pretty or that your boots have no tread? In either case, call it an educated guess."

"You . . . you're . . . you're *unbelievable*!" Tiffany sputtered, though she didn't twist out of his arms. She was under the influence of a strange lassitude that kept her right where she was. "First you make fun of me, then you issue orders like some drill sergeant, then you . . . you start *mauling* me," she grumbled.

"I'm not mauling you. I'm cuddling you. I like the way you nestle in. Besides, who fell into whose arms?"

Damn. He was right. She *had* nestled in. "It was an unfortunate accident," she said, stiffening her body.

"An accident that wouldn't have happened if you'd waited inside the way you were told," Mitch pointed out.

Tiffany closed her eyes and counted to ten. "I'm not sure what kind of yes-women you're used to dealing with, Mr. Canfield," she said at last, speaking in careful syllables as if to someone who didn't know the language very well. "But this particular female doesn't always do what she's told."

"You know, I could've guessed that." Mitch tightened his arms in a hug that was pure insolence. "But you'd better learn to take advice, at least until you've mastered the art of staying on your feet and out of trouble in these parts. Lesson number one, for instance: Don't stick your nose in the air when you should be watching where you're walking. And number two: When a gentleman saves you from a bruised behind, it's nice to thank him."

Tiffany was properly chastised. He was right again. "Thank you for saving me from a . . . a nasty tumble," she said primly. "But must you be so patronizing?"

He laughed and released her, though he kept one hand curved under her elbow to hold her steady while he guided her to the car. "You're right, and I apologize. However, I have to tell you—without being patronizing, of course—that you need to get better equipped for the weather here, preferably before you go to the farm. Decent boots and much warmer clothes should be your top priority. You don't even have a hat."

"Neither do you."

"I have a cap in my pocket. I'm not wearing it at the moment, but it's never very far from me. Same thing with gloves. Good warm gloves, though. Those unlined leather jobs of yours are as useless against the cold as those shiny black boots and that daffodil coat."

Tiffany grudgingly agreed. Without his arms keeping her warm and his body sheltering her from the wind, she was freezing—her ears, her face, her fingers, her toes, her whole body. And she hadn't realized how smooth the soles of her boots were. Perhaps she should listen to what he had to say, at least until she was acclimatized.

They reached the car, and he opened the door. "Get in," he ordered.

"Yes, *sir*!" Tiffany retorted. So much for his apology. "What did you think I was planning to do? Ride on the front fender?"

He bent down to make sure her coattail wouldn't get caught in the door. "You can be a sarcastic little thing, can't you?"

Tiffany, at five seven, hadn't been called a "little thing" since about the age of six. She was too taken aback to show him how sarcastic she could be if she put her mind to it.

"Use the seat belt," Mitch said as he straightened up. "We have laws here."

"Believe it or not, other places have laws too," she said sweetly. "I always do up my seat belt."

"Good. That's one less habit you'll have to acquire," he said, then grinned at her and closed the door.

Tiffany found her own mouth twitching, threatening again to curve in an outright smile. The man was outrageous and impossible, but she knew she deserved his teasing. She was a rank tenderfoot who'd been too cowardly to find out exactly what she was walking into. If their positions were reversed, she wasn't sure she would be able to resist kidding him.

"I'd almost forgotten that this is Sunday," she said when Mitch climbed in behind the wheel of the Jeep. "Are there any stores open so I can get more suitable clothes? I'm authorized to buy what I need and put it on expenses. And since you seem to be pressed for time, you could drop me off at a mall. I'll grab a taxi to get to your brother's farm."

"I'm not in a hurry now. I didn't want a parking ticket, that's all. They're a nuisance." Mitch put the Jeep in gear and negotiated it out of its spot. "I'll take you to a shop where you'll get wholesale prices. Once you're outfitted, we'll head for the farm."

Tiffany was taken aback. "That's very kind of you," she said, realizing only after she'd spoken that she sounded astonished.

He laughed good-naturedly, then gave her a slow, sexy smile. "My pleasure."

His words, his tone, his whole manner reminded Tiffany of the unsettling moments when she'd been in his arms, and an unwelcome thrill skittered up her spine. She suspected he'd meant to accomplish that. Mitch Canfield obviously knew his effect on women. His type always did. "Honestly, I wouldn't mind taking a cab," she said with a touch of panic. "I'm sure you have more important things to—"

"Out of the question," he cut in firmly.

Tiffany shook her head. Was there any end to his arbitrary pronouncements? She opened her mouth to deliver a few pungent, overdue comments about his dictatorial tendencies.

"By the way," he said before she could utter a word, "what were you doing at the car rental counter?"

She scowled at him, thrown off stride. "What do people usually do at a car rental counter? When no one showed up to meet me, I decided to arrange for a car."

"You were planning to drive to the farm on your own?"

"Why not? I can read a map. I'd have found my way."

"Have you ever coped with winter road conditions?"

"No, but I've handled my share of dune buggies on sandy beaches. How different can snow be?"

Mitch laughed as if she'd said something hilarious. "Tiffany, give the unsuspecting drivers of Winnipeg a break. Don't test that theory."

She chose not to argue the point. The man was insufferable, but she couldn't deny that he was trying to be thoughtful, helpful, and cheerful in his own irritating way. It wasn't Mitch's fault that she had very little patience with cocky, know-it-all, flirtatious males.

What she couldn't understand was why this one attracted her. Had her immunity worn off, like an old vaccination?

"How long do you expect to stay here?" Mitch asked.

"I'm not sure," Tiffany answered cautiously, wondering why he wanted to know. Was he trying to find out whether she was predisposed to recommending the proposed share-purchase?

He didn't accept her vague reply. "Do you have any idea? A day? A week? Longer?"

"I really don't know. For the time being, I'll need only enough clothes for a couple of days."

"And if my brother and Jackie make an arrangement with the company you work for, are you likely to stick around?"

"Why do you ask?"

He glanced over at her with a familiar twinkle in his eyes and a devilish grin lifting one corner of his mouth. "Just curious."

All at once Tiffany felt extremely uncomfortable. And warm. Much too warm. She was certain he'd given her fair warning that he was interested in her, that he intended to follow up on that interest if given the opportunity, and that he was confident she would find him difficult to resist. Yet she couldn't tell him to back off, because he hadn't said or done anything she could call an outright come-on. "Unless you're keeping your car heater going full blast for yourself, you could turn it down now," she suggested in a strained voice.

"Good," he said, immediately adjusting the fan. "I was almost at the well-done stage. Now, to go back to your question, the reason I asked how long you planned to stay was to find out whether I should take you out for a few driving lessons so you could get around on your own without being a gas-propelled torpedo."

"Oh," Tiffany said, wondering if she'd imagined the sexual challenge she'd sensed a moment earlier. "Well, that's very nice," she murmured.

He reached over and patted her tightly folded hands. "I'm a nice guy. Didn't you spot my sterling qualities right away?"

Tiffany burst out laughing. "You're a rogue, Mitch Canfield. But let's get one thing straight right now: I don't mix business and pleasure."

His grin turned even more wicked, the gleam in his eyes more devilish. "Thanks for the compliment."

"What compliment? You're flattered to be called a rogue?"

"No, I'm flattered to be referred to as a pleasure."

Tiffany's mouth opened, then closed. She pressed her lips firmly together, learning fast that anything she said could be held against her.

TWO

Tiffany was puzzled as Mitch pulled into a small strip mall and stopped in front of a sports equipment store. "Nothing here looks open," she said, wondering why he couldn't see for himself that the lights were off in most of the mall's shops and there didn't seem to be anyone inside.

Mitch smiled and got out of the Jeep. "This time, sit tight until I come around for you."

Tiffany sat tight. The last thing she needed was to get out of the Jeep, slip on the treacherous ground, and fall into his arms again. "What are we going to do?" she asked when he opened the door on her side and extended his hand to her. "Break a window?"

"We could try that," Mitch said, his fingers closing around hers. Jingling his keys in his free hand, he added, "Or we could go in the easy way."

Tiffany hesitated and looked up at the Canfield

Sports sign, then laughed as she stepped down onto the ground in the narrow space between Mitch and the car. Instead of moving back to make more room for her, he stayed where he was, disturbingly close. "Of course," he said softly, "if you entertain racy fantasies about being half of a team of cat burglars . . ."

"My racy fantasies are none of your business."

Mitch laughed and tugged on her hand to haul her to his side, then pushed the car door shut. "At least you admit you *have* racy fantasies. That's refreshing honesty in a woman."

She looked up at him with sudden wariness. "Is it really necessary for you to hold on to me this way?"

"Until you're wearing better boots, yes."

Sighing in resignation, she gave up arguing.

Once inside the store, Tiffany was surprised by its size. It extended a long way back and branched out to form an L shape. "You own all this?" she asked, impressed.

"The stock and the display fixtures, yes. The real estate, no." Leading Tiffany toward the rear of the store, Mitch looked around as if seeing the place for the first time. "It's getting out of hand, though. I had to rent that extra wing last year, and we're bursting at the seams again."

Following him into the wing, Tiffany saw a colorful array of winter sportswear. "You must be tremendously successful. Why did you tell me you were a ski bum?"

"I didn't. That was your idea. I said it was a good

guess, and it was. I'm a ski bum at heart." He looked around the store again, frowning. "What started as a small enterprise to keep me in lift passes has taken off like a rocket."

Tiffany couldn't understand why he seemed less than pleased. "Is there something wrong with success?"

"Plenty. It uses up too much time and energy." His frown abruptly changed to the beguiling grin Tiffany was already starting to recognize as a challenge, his way of silently saying that he made his own rules, lived his life exactly as he chose, and had no intention of changing his ways.

He stepped in behind her and lightly rested his hands on her shoulders while she undid her coat buttons. "I'll take your coat," he said.

Tiffany hastily shrugged out of it. Mitch's nearness was triggering the troubling sensations she'd experienced at the airport, and his touch was electric even when it was innocent. "What would you prefer to do with your life?" she asked, hoping he wouldn't notice the slight breathlessness in her voice.

"Enjoy it, mainly," he answered, moving away to hang her coat on one of the display racks. He took off his own jacket and tossed it over the top of the rack. "Who knows? I might sell everything one of these days to buy back my freedom." As he turned to Tiffany, his gaze was frankly admiring.

She wished she'd worn something besides a scarlet sweater-dress that skimmed over her body to a hemline well above her knees. It had seemed like a comfortable choice for the long flight and businesslike enough for her first meeting with the Canfields, but all at once she felt exposed and a little too . . . well . . . sexy. "And what will you do after you've sold out?" she asked, trying to put the unnerving Mr. Canfield on the defensive. "Ski until the money's gone and you have to start over?"

Mitch grinned at her. "Sounds like a pretty good plan."

Tiffany couldn't believe her ears. For a man to build up a profitable venture and then joke about tossing it aside for the sake of a perpetual ski holiday was inconceivable. "Don't you have any ambition at all?" she asked, moving to one of the racks of jackets to riffle through them.

"I have plenty of ambition. There's a whole world of mountains out there, for instance, and I want to schuss down as many as I can before I get sent off to that big ski chalet in the sky."

Tiffany looked over her shoulder at him. "That big ski chalet in the sky? Tell me you didn't say that."

He laughed. "Okay, so I get a little corny when I talk about the great passion of my life. What are you looking for, Tiffany?"

Absently examining a lime-green jacket as if considering trying it on, Tiffany answered carefully, "The same as most people. A certain amount of satisfaction in my work, whatever sense of personal security I can find, and enough moments of pleasure along the way to make the whole effort worthwhile."

"A reasonable philosophy," Mitch commented. "But all I was asking was what you were looking for on that rack of jackets."

She whirled and glared at him. "Something warm to wear, of course," she said. "Isn't that what we're here for?"

"Then I suggest we skip the men's section and go straight to the women's." Mitch's lips twitched with a suppressed smile as he waved a hand toward a display unit behind him.

Tiffany stayed where she was, folding her arms over her middle and cocking her head to one side to give him a long, measuring look. "You love doing that, don't you?"

"Doing what?"

"Keeping a person off center."

"Only some persons," he said, turning to look through a row of women's jackets.

"Why me?"

He pulled out a hot pink ski jacket with black trim and held it up to check it with Tiffany's coloring. "Maybe because you're so earnest. You seem to take life so seriously, I can't resist having a little fun with you. And there's that pugnacious chin of yours. I love watching it snap up and jut out. How about trying this one on for size?"

"Life *is* serious," she countered, taking the jacket

and slipping it on. "But I think you simply like to keep the upper hand, especially with women."

"Could be. With desirable women, anyway. There are a lot of Delilahs out there waiting to give a man the old short-back-and-sides, you know."

"Poor baby," Tiffany murmured with a tiny smile. She had no idea whether Mitch was revealing genuine wariness of the entire female sex or just putting her on. In either case, she was ready to drop the subject. It had become unsafe the moment he'd implied that she was a desirable woman.

Stepping over to a mirror, she looked at herself and made a face. "The jacket seems to fit. Is there a bottom half?"

"Coming right up," Mitch said. When he handed her a padded nylon pair of ski pants, she wrinkled up her nose. "What's with the astronaut look?"

"Believe me, I'd suggest formfitting stirrup pants if my conscience would allow it, but you'll need serious warmth for the tearing around you'll be doing at the farm. By the way, I hope you've brought some jeans and sweaters." Mitch's glance flickered over her again, warming her body like a heat-throwing ray gun. "For the next couple of days you won't have much use for chic little dresses like the one you're wearing."

"I do have jeans in my suitcase, but I figured I could buy a sweater after I got here," she said, wishing again that she were wearing something—anything—but the red knit dress he seemed so intrigued by. Asbestos coveralls, maybe.

"A sweater," he repeated absently, then nodded. "Right. A sweater. I can look after that too. How about underwear?"

Tiffany's eyes widened. "Are you this personal with all your customers?"

"I'm talking about the thermal kind," Mitch said, chuckling at her indignation. He went to a wall shelf, sorted through the packages on it, and made his selection.

She took a step backward as he thrust two packages at her, as if he were proffering a basket of serpents.

"Pure silk," he said, opening one package and removing an elegant jersey. "You've never felt anything more luxurious against your skin. Will you give it a try?"

She took the top. "Any special fitting room?"

"Take your pick," he said, pointing to the row of stalls. "But first . . ." He clamped his hands down on her shoulders, marched her toward a chair, and sat her down.

"*Now* what?" she asked as he knelt in front of her.

"You can't try on clothes without taking off your boots," he said, cupping his hands under one of her heels and pulling.

Tiffany sighed and cooperated. When he'd tugged her boot halfway off, he curved one hand around the top of her calf while pulling the boot the rest of the way with the other. It occurred to her that she should have told him she could manage by herself. There was a dangerous intimacy in what he was doing. She felt too much warmth in his palm. Too much gentle strength in his fingers. Too much electricity in his touch. Wild, sensual visions popped into her mind, and she had to battle them away. Transfixed, she wondered whether he was experiencing the same sensations.

Setting the boot aside, he suddenly looked up at her. As his eyes met hers, his hand glided slowly down to her ankle before lowering her foot to the floor.

Tiffany caught her breath and couldn't muster a protest, couldn't tear her gaze from his. He lifted her other leg, tugged on the boot, and again curved his hand around the top of her calf, his fingertips lightly brushing a sensitive spot at the back of her knee.

She wasn't certain whether he was being deliberately provocative or not, so she chose not to challenge him. To her surprise, he was the one who ultimately ended the charged silence, giving his head a tiny but visible shake as he stood up. "Now you can go into the fitting room," he said, his voice oddly strained. "Meanwhile, I'll find a sweater and some boots."

"Fine," she said distractedly as she stood up. Had she glimpsed a side of the man he hadn't meant her to see? Had his teasing flirtatiousness backfired? For a few moments, had they both been caught up in a strange spell?

She blinked herself back to reality. Jet lag, she told herself as she escaped to the nearest cubicle to change her mood along with her clothes. She was being foolish. She knew perfectly well that the fleeting intensity of Mitch Canfield's expression was part of his act. He was a ladies' man, with dozens of charming tricks up his sleeve.

Alarm bells were going off in her mind, and experience had taught her to listen to them.

Mitch was lost in thought as he selected a brightly patterned sweater for Tiffany. He couldn't figure himself out. It wasn't like him to find one excuse after another to touch a woman—especially a woman he'd just met, a woman who was visiting his family for professional reasons.

Still, for all the knee-high leather boots he'd helped remove in his day, he'd never experienced the powerful rush he'd felt when the sleek curve of Tiffany's calves had been in his hands. And when her soft green eyes had mirrored her startled response, he'd been within an inch of taking her in his arms and tasting her inviting lips. Nothing quite as potent as that moment had ever happened to him before—except perhaps when the same woman had fallen into his arms outside the airport terminal. He'd had to come up with a quick, flippant excuse for not letting go of her.

Damn, he thought as he looked through the selection of boots to find a sensible pair for Tiffany. Wanting a woman was normal enough, but something else was going on here. He was having trouble remembering that he barely knew Tiffany Greer. He felt too comfortable with her—in an extremely uncomfortable way—which made no sense at all. She wasn't his type.

He found a pair of colorful boots, grabbed some

warm socks, and took them back to the fitting room. "How's it going?" he asked through the closed door.

"Fine. The pants fit, and you're right about this silk," she said, sounding unexpectedly enthusiastic. "The fabric is fabulous. Are you sure it's meant for warmth? It seems too decadent to be practical."

"I'm positive," Mitch answered, smiling. "You've had another lesson in coping with the north. Practicality and pleasure can go hand in hand. I have something else for you to put on."

Tiffany opened the cubicle door. "Thanks," she said, accepting the sweater, her brows raised in apparent surprise as she added, "It's beautiful! You have wonderful taste."

"Glad you like it," Mitch said, frowning. The silk underwear top, clinging to her like a second skin, revealed the lacy outline of a bra that cupped lovely breasts, just full enough to spill sweetly into a man's waiting hands, and the emerald shade brought out gemlike glints in her soft green eyes. Her hair was more tousled than before, and her skin was slightly flushed. He watched, mesmerized, as she pulled on the sweater.

"What do you think?" she asked brightly, finger-combing her hair after the sweater was in place.

That you look the way you would after lovemaking, he thought. "It'll do," he muttered, then held out the boots he'd chosen for her. "Try these now."

Tiffany still looked dubious, but she sat down in the chair to give them a try.

"You're a good sport," Mitch said as he put the

boots on the floor beside her and handed her the socks.

"Don't bet on it. If I find out that this is some initiation thing where you get me all decked out in a ridiculous outfit and everybody else is in normal clothes, I'll find a way to lure you back to Hawaii and feed you to my pet shark."

She could lure him anywhere, he mused, but said only, "You have a pet shark?"

"Why, sure. Everybody in Hawaii has a pet shark. 'Course, it's only the tenderfeet from the mainland who try to pet them." She grinned. "Once."

Mitch laughed and left her to try on the boots without his help while he picked up some accessories. When he heard a peal of laughter, he turned to see Tiffany standing in front of a mirror in full regalia.

"Come on, admit it," she said. "You're doing a number on me. I've watched the Winter Olympics on television. Nobody looks like this."

"Maybe not, but take it from me, sweetheart. Olympic competitors don't have to deal with the icy winds that whip across the fields of an open prairie," Mitch pointed out.

"But I can't walk properly," she protested. "Look. I waddle." She demonstrated.

"Never mind, it's a cute waddle," Mitch said, realizing too late that he was flirting again. It was hard not to. She did have a cute waddle.

She walked a little farther, starting and stopping. "I make noises when I move," she said, taking another step. "Listen. I rustle. I swish."

"Everybody does. It's the fabric."

"Well, I feel silly. I'm not used to rustling and swishing."

"After a while, you won't even notice it," Mitch reassured her. "Why don't you swish on over here, and we'll complete your ensemble?"

She shot him a look of mock horror, but went to him. "You mean there's more?"

"Just a little," Mitch said, handing her a thick wool cap in an abstract hot pink and black design.

She put it on and smiled. "The color coordination is perfect. Are we finished yet?"

He gave her a pair of fleece-lined nylon mittens and wrapped a black scarf around her neck, grinning as he tugged it up over her nose. "Now we're finished. This is the way you have to dress when you're touring the facilities on the farm."

"Can I put my other clothes back on for now?"

"If you wish. I'll go outside and warm up the Jeep."

Tiffany pulled down the scarf so she could look. "Aren't you forgetting something?" she said as he headed for the door, grabbing his jacket on the way. "Like the bill?"

Mitch was in a hurry to get out of the store. Tiffany was entirely too delectable in her new look, and the thought of slowly peeling off layer after layer to get down to her alluring femininity was heady stuff. "I'll make out a bill in the morning and drop it off at the farm sometime in the next couple of days," he said, hastily putting on his jacket.

"All right, but forget that thing you said earlier about giving me wholesale prices. I don't want you to be cheated of your profit." Tiffany grinned. "A small corporate discount would be more than generous, thank you."

Zipping up his jacket, Mitch returned to her and couldn't resist giving her pert nose a gentle tweak. "I like your style, Tiffany Greer. And you look great in that outfit. Anyone would think you'd been born for the north country."

"What a horrible thought," Tiffany said with a groan, but smiled as she clomped her way back to the fitting room in her strange new boots. She couldn't understand why anyone would choose to live in a place that involved such complicated preparations just to go outside, yet she was beginning to think she might be able to handle this assignment as an adventure. It would be a story she could tell her grandchildren while they built sandcastles on a South Pacific beach.

Inside the cubicle, she saw her flushed cheeks and a special brightness in her eyes, and she placed a forefinger lightly on the tip of her nose. It tingled where Mitch had touched it.

She heaved a sigh and told herself that if she really hoped to look back on this experience someday and laugh, she'd better be on guard against that charming, handsome, would-be ski bum who undoubtedly had a girl in every hilltop village from the Rockies to the Alps.

Back in Hawaii among the surfing set, she'd learned to spot a heartbreaker as well as an ocean breaker when she saw one. Like the big waves, Mitch Canfield might offer an exhilarating ride, but any woman who tried that one was in for a serious wipeout.

THREE

Tiffany shaded her eyes and squinted against the glare of sun on the snow. As the Jeep left the city limits and headed along a country road bounded by endless white fields, she envied Mitch his Ray-Bans.

"Don't you have dark glasses with you?" he asked.

"I left them at home," she said, surprised that he'd noticed her discomfort. His whole attention seemed to be focused on keeping the car centered on the deep tire grooves that had been worn into the packed ice and snow on the road. "It was dumb of me, I know, but I figured I wouldn't need them up here."

"It wasn't dumb of you. It was a natural mistake. I should have thought about sunglasses back at the store." He reached over and popped open the glove compartment. "I usually carry extras . . . Good. Here they are." He took out a pair of sunglasses and handed them to Tiffany.

Putting them on, Tiffany found instant relief. "They're great. All of a sudden I understand snow blindness. Even the sky is such a clear, brilliant blue, it hurts."

Mitch glanced at her with a satisfied expression. "We boast about our sunny skies. People who leave for milder climates as often as not come scurrying back when they discover they'd rather put up with the cold than with weeks of gray, dismal, rainy days."

"You honestly love this place," Tiffany said, amazed.

"When I'm here, yes. When I'm in Switzerland, that's the greatest place in the world. The same goes for the Caribbean, New York City"—he winked at her—"or even Hawaii."

She laughed, more from nervousness than amusement. From Mitch, even an obvious male ploy like a casual wink aroused odd stirrings inside her. She hated being so susceptible. "So, to paraphrase the old song, when you're not in the place you love, you love the place you're in?" she said lightly.

"Exactly."

"Does the same thing hold true for the actual lyrics? When you're not near the girl you love, you love the girl you're near?" Tiffany almost bit off her tongue, but it was too late. The question was out, hanging in the air between them, mocking her.

For several moments, Mitch didn't respond, lapsing into his own private thoughts. Unhappy thoughts, Tiffany mused, forgetting her embarrassment as she saw the sudden tightness in his jaw. She wished she could see his eyes. But before she could concoct a romantic tragedy in his past, he turned to her with the grin that was guaranteed to rile her. "Let's just say I tend to live for the moment. Do you have any special reason for asking?"

She refused to be bested. "I'm the girl you're near at the moment, remember? I need to know whether I should keep my brass knuckles handy."

He laughed as if he enjoyed her comebacks. "You're safe, Tiffany. Big brother would have my head on a platter if I didn't behave myself. A lot of research went into choosing the company you work for as their preferred joint-venture partner, and I'm not going to risk clouding the issue by trying to start something with you, tempting as that prospect is."

"Have you any idea why they're favoring Paradise Foods?" Tiffany asked, resolutely ignoring his last comment and sticking to the safer ground of business talk.

"Market positioning, ethics, long-term goals— several factors are involved. Let me toss the question back at you. Why does a Hawaiian firm want to buy into one in Winnipeg?"

"We have subsidiaries and partnerships all over the continent, and the products coming out of Canfield Farm seem to fit right in with the others."

"How did you get to be the person who makes such important decisions? You seem pretty young for that much responsibility."

"I'm not all that young," Tiffany said with an edge of impatience. "I'm twenty-six. I have an M.B.A. and I've been with Paradise Foods since I finished grad school, so it's not as if I'm untrained or inexperienced. I don't make the decisions, though. Just recommendations. And this is my first solo project."

"Which is why you're willing to come to the winter-ravaged boondocks," Mitch commented. "Paying your dues, are you?"

Tiffany nodded and answered casually, "I hope to prove myself, yes."

"So you're caught between a rock and a hard place."

"What do you mean?"

"The way I understand it, if you recommend going ahead with a merger, you'll have to settle in the Great White North for a while. If you deep-six it, you'll get to go home, but you'll have lost your chance to prove yourself."

Although Tiffany had been acutely aware of that dilemma for some time, she bristled at hearing it spelled out in such uncompromising terms. "I believe I can make my recommendation objectively," she said with a lift of her chin.

Mitch glanced over at her, his brows raised. "All of a sudden the chill factor in here is worse than outside. I didn't mean to suggest you'd let personal considerations enter into your decision, Ms. Greer. I'm sure that your personal considerations always run a poor second to professional ones."

Tiffany was sure his last remark wasn't intended as a compliment, but she didn't get the chance to challenge him about it. Her heart suddenly leapt to her throat. A pickup truck was careening toward them after making a too-fast turn from a side road. It was out of control, its rear end fishtailing as the driver struggled to get the wheels settled into the deep ruts. Tiffany reflexively braced her feet against the floorboards.

She was stunned when Mitch tromped down on the gas pedal, at the same time wrenching the steering wheel hard to the right. The Jeep bounced out of the grooved tracks and onto the snow-packed shoulder just as the truck, still swerving wildly, flashed by.

Tiffany's heart was pounding and her fingers were digging into her palms. She stared at Mitch in astonishment. He'd managed to avoid a collision that had seemed certain, and was as cool as an Indy champion.

Easing up on the gas, he gradually maneuvered the Cherokee back onto the road and into the ruts, then glanced into the rearview mirror. "Good," he said calmly. "That half-ton's under control. I thought I was going to have to turn around and dig it out of a snowbank."

"Good lord," Tiffany whispered. No wonder Mitch had laughed at her plan to drive herself to the farm. "Does this sort of thing happen often?"

He glanced at her and smiled. "What sort of thing?"

Leaning back against the headrest and closing her eyes, Tiffany counted to a hundred. Mitch Canfield had probably saved her life, but if she got to the farm without strangling him, it was going to be a miracle.

Any mental image Tiffany had been harboring of Old MacDonald's ramshackle homestead was banished as the Cherokee reached the top of a gentle rise and Mitch indicated a wide panorama of snow-covered fields. "We're here," he said casually. "Canfield Farm. Both sides of the road, as far as the eye can see and quite a bit beyond."

"Heavens, it's enormous," Tiffany murmured. "And beautiful," she added, taking in the picturesque clumps of evergreens with thick dollops of snow weighing down their boughs, the groups of buildings nestled here and there in a Christmas-card setting, the large white house trimmed with gleaming black shutters and nestled far back from the road behind a graceful arrangement of stately, bare-branched trees. "It's just lovely," she said softly, then looked at Mitch and smiled. "I'd call it cozy if I didn't know how cold it is out there—and if it weren't so huge."

Mitch grinned at her, a glint of pride as well as the usual teasing sparkle in his eyes. "What did you expect? A vegetable patch with Peter Rabbit peeking out from behind a moth-eaten cabbage?"

"Hardly," Tiffany said, laughing. "But I hadn't pictured a place that looked like a sprawling ranch in Texas."

"Texas? That postage stamp piece of real estate?

Hell, we could put two or three Lone Star States in Manitoba, and probably have room left over for all of New England."

"And you exaggerate as well as any Texan," Tiffany shot back.

Mitch chuckled and eased the Jeep through a left turn onto a long road that led up to the house. "I don't see the van," he commented. "I guess the family isn't back yet."

"You never did tell me why your brother couldn't meet me at the airport," Tiffany said. "Has something come up that makes my being here an inconvenience?"

"Don't get your hopes up. Something came up, but it won't give you an excuse to hightail it back to the South Seas. Pete and Jackie had to take their son to the emergency room, that's all."

"That's all?"

"It's nothing to make a fuss about. Danny needed his eyebrow sewn up after a skate blade clipped him during a hockey game. Just a normal little slice with a lot of blood, no serious damage."

Following a circular driveway in front of the house, Mitch pulled up almost to the door, then switched off the ignition and turned to her with a smile. "Are you a hockey fan?"

"We don't have a lot of ice rinks in Hawaii."

Mitch unfastened his seat belt. "Shall we go inside and continue our conversation beside a nice warm fire?"

Tiffany's forehead creased in a worried frown. "Is it all right? I mean, do you live here?"

"Not now, but it's my second home, and I have a key. Wait here while I go unlock the place. That way you won't have to spend any more time out in the cold than necessary."

As Mitch got out of the Jeep and strode up the walk to the door of the farmhouse, Tiffany mused that he probably had an extensive collection of keys. He was the type who would have them pressed into his palm by eager ladies all the time.

The thought left her feeling strangely bleak.

Mitch returned and opened her door, and the instant she stepped out of the Jeep she was certain her lungs were being quick-frozen. Struggling for breath, she turned her face into Mitch's shoulder as he wrapped an arm around her and rushed her toward the house. The packed snow squeaked under their boots, and the wind lashed at her legs like a bullwhip. Tiffany thought about the weather she'd left behind, and suddenly the whole situation seemed as ludicrous as a slapstick comedy. By the time they were safely inside the house with the door shut behind them, she collapsed against it, giggling helplessly.

Mitch watched her for a moment, then cupped the nape of her neck with one hand, her chin with the other. "Tiffany Greer," he said quietly, "that infectious laugh of yours could make a man forget his scruples."

Her smile faded quickly as she looked up at him.

She ordered herself to move away from him before the amber flames in the depths of his eyes completely hypnotized her, but her body ignored the command. As he slid his arms around her, enveloping her in his warmth, her hands found their way to his chest and rested there, unresisting.

Aware of a peculiar, otherworldly hush, as if the snow outside cushioned every sound, Tiffany was spellbound, held captive by Mitch's steady gaze as he slowly lowered his head until his mouth was moving over hers.

His lips were warm and firm, his kiss gently persuasive, neither demanding nor impatient. Tiffany felt herself slipping into a dreamlike trance as his tongue lightly caressed her lips, coaxed them apart, and slowly circled their moist inner flesh. The tantalizing, sweet taste of him affected her like a sip of potent brandy. Liquid heat coiled through her body, melting resistance, dissolving inhibition, leaving her with a blissful, floating sensation. It was a slow, deliciously thorough kiss, a kiss that made her legs weak, her body soft and pliant. Her heart pounded wildly. Her fingers crept to the back of his neck and sifted through his hair. Her tongue sought his as a languid heaviness settled between her thighs.

A soft moan of desire from deep in her own throat shocked her back to her senses. Dropping her hands to Mitch's shoulders, she pushed him away and twisted out of his arms. As she hastily put a few paces between them, she smoothed her hair and managed a ragged laugh. "You said I'd be safe with you."

"Unfortunately, I didn't consider whether *I'd* be safe with *you*," he said, sounding genuinely shaken.

"I never thought I'd say this in a frigid climate, but can we cool it from now on?" she suggested.

"We'd better," Mitch agreed, his manner unexpectedly subdued. "There are kisses, and there are kisses. That one was in a class by itself."

Tiffany kept a smile glued to her lips. "I admit you're quite an expert," she said, refusing to take him seriously.

"Expertise had nothing to do with it," he countered.

"Expertise had everything to do with it." She abruptly changed the subject. "Didn't you say something about building a fire?" She cranked up the voltage of her smile. "In the fireplace, that is."

After gazing at her with unnerving intensity for several long moments, Mitch visibly lightened up and reverted to his usual teasing form. "Don't worry, Tiffany. I'll light your fire as soon as I've brought your things in from the Cherokee," he said, his eyes once again alight with challenge. "Just let me take your coat . . ."

"I think I'd like to keep my coat on for a few more minutes," she said, folding her arms over her middle and hugging herself. She wasn't chilly; the house was comfortably warm. She simply didn't want Mitch to touch her again. The effect he had on her was alarming. "I'll wait here and open the door when you come back with the suitcases," she suggested, knowing it would be an empty gesture to offer to go back outside with him. He would only order her to stay put.

A few minutes later, when he'd brought in the suitcases, he said, "I'll make one more trip to get the bags of clothes we took from the store and to move the Jeep around to the side of the house, and then I'll get that fire going."

Tiffany watched him through a long, vertical pane of glass beside the door, wondering if her superiors back in Honolulu had any concept of the conditions they expected her to cope with.

After a few minutes, when she saw Mitch striding up the walk, her pulse raced and her lips parted as if inviting another of his long, lovely kisses. "Good lord, what have I gotten myself into?" she blurted out. Horrified as she was by the realities of the climate, she was even more appalled by the fact that she'd been charmed out of her wits by a wolf in ski bum's clothing within minutes of having met him. She simply had to regain control of the situation. And of herself. Fast.

She opened the door as Mitch was stamping his feet on the hemp mat outside. He stepped in and quickly shut the door behind him. Tiffany tried not to find him overwhelmingly appealing, but the scent he exuded was so clean and fresh, so distinctly masculine, she was assailed by a wild temptation to throw her arms around him and nuzzle into his throat.

Come on, you ninny, get a grip, she reminded herself as she backed away from him.

Mitch took off his jacket, hung it on an antique hat

stand chair, and sat down to unlace his boots. "Maybe I should take your gear up to your room before I build that fire."

"You know which room is mine?" Tiffany asked, peering into the Canfield Sports bags as if to make sure all the clothes she'd bought were there, though she was simply trying not to look at Mitch. It wasn't easy to insulate herself against his impact.

"Jackie told me she was putting you in my room," he said, kicking off his boots and standing up.

Tiffany's head snapped up. "*Your* room?"

"Sorry, I mean the room that used to be mine." He gave her a crooked, teasing smile. "Don't worry, Tiffany. I grew up on the farm, but I have my own house in town. My room here has been made over for guests, and when I spend the occasional night here in my old bed, I'm just another guest." He sighed theatrically, pretending sad nostalgia, then shot her a questioning look. "You weren't thinking that I meant you'd be expected to share accommodations with me, were you?"

"Hardly," Tiffany said, forcing a smile, wishing she knew what it was about Mitch Canfield that had her at sixes and sevens. The mere thought of sleeping in his bed, even if it wasn't his bed anymore, was enough to hamper her breathing.

"Are you ready to give up your coat and boots now?" he asked.

Tiffany stared blankly at him. Her lively imagination had climbed into his bed and was still there, inhaling the spicy scent of his pillows, enjoying the smoothness of his crisp sheets against her skin, watching him stretch out beside her, both of them shamelessly naked.

"The house isn't that cold," Mitch said, giving her a quizzical look. "You can curl up in one of the chairs in front of the fireplace. I'll give you an afghan to tuck around you."

Tiffany finally came back to reality. "That'd be nice, thanks. Sorry if I seem vague. I was . . . admiring the house."

Hastily taking off her coat, she started to put it on one of the hat stand hooks, but Mitch reached for it and hung it in the closet. "Sit down and I'll help you with your boots."

Tiffany hesitated. She wouldn't go any farther inside with her boots on, but she didn't want a repeat of what had happened back at the store.

"No hanky-panky," he said, reading her mind. "Promise."

With a fleeting smile, she sat down and stuck out one leg.

Mitch was as good as his word. Her boots were off in no time, without so much as a meaningful glance. "Do you want to get settled in with that afghan now, or would you prefer to go upstairs and see your room?" he asked as she stood up.

She suspected that it wasn't a wise plan to enter any bedroom with Mitch, but as her glance took in all the parcels as well as her suitcases, she knew she couldn't play princess and sit around while he carried everything upstairs. "I'll go with you," she said, picking up the plastic bags.

Mitch gave her another odd little smile, as if he knew exactly what was going on in her mind, then grabbed her suitcases and led the way to the stairs straight ahead.

Forcing herself to think about something besides Mitch's inexplicable effect on her, Tiffany carefully looked everywhere but at his lean hips and taut thighs as she followed him up the steps. She concentrated on what she could see of the house—the spacious entry bounded by a formal dining room on the left and an inviting living room on the right.

The look was country casual, with high ceilings, hardwood floors accented with area rugs, and walls painted rich, intense colors or papered with traditional floral patterns.

The guest room was a place where anyone could feel comfortable, its forest-green walls a dramatic backdrop for natural pine furnishings, shuttered windows, and an abstract print comforter. The one feminine touch was a pretty floral arrangement in a white ceramic jug on the dresser. "What a lovely bouquet," she commented.

Mitch put the suitcases on a low bench at the foot of the bed, then turned to Tiffany with one of his winning smiles. "You like the flowers? I'm glad. I picked 'em myself."

"You did?" Tiffany said, grateful that he was trying

to recapture their playful, prekiss mood. "Where? How?"

Lights flashed and twinkled in his eyes. "You haven't heard of the Manitoba Winter-Blooming Snowflower?"

She shot him a dubious look as she opened one of the suitcases to take out a pair of black leather pumps. "Funny, they look like roses to me."

"Of course they look like roses. That's one of the snowflower's most striking characteristics," Mitch said in a serious, professorial tone as he bent down to sniff one of the blossoms. "They even smell like roses. But I don't think you'd find roses growing under the snow out behind the barn."

"Under the snow?" Tiffany said with mock gravity as she slipped her feet into the pumps. "How fascinating."

Mitch straightened up and nodded. "Deep under the snow. The deeper, the better. It protects them from the cold, but it makes it quite an art to find them."

"I'd say you're master of another art, as well," Tiffany said, sitting on the edge of the bed to test it.

"What art would that be?"

She stood up, walked over to him, and poked her index finger into his chest. "The art of the snow job."

He laughed, but his amusement faded abruptly as he curled his fingers around her hand. "Dammit, Tiffany, do you have to be such a delight to be with?"

She tugged back her hand and moved away from him, a flush stealing over her throat and face. "Maybe we should go back downstairs now," she suggested in a strained voice.

After a brief hesitation, Mitch nodded. "There's no 'maybe' about it," he said, then sighed dramatically. "And when we get there, Tiffany Greer, you stay away from me, you hear?"

Her laugh was forced. "I'll do my best," she promised. But even as he stepped back to let her leave the room ahead of him, she had to resist his raw physical magnetism on the way by.

She only hoped the rest of the Canfields would show up soon. If ever there was a need for a rescue party to save a lost soul on the frozen tundra, this was it.

FOUR

Tiffany quickly decided there was something to be said for nestling into an overstuffed chair beside a crackling fireplace while the wind outside howled and whistled constant reminders of how snug she was.

With her shoes kicked off, and her feet tucked under her, she sipped cocoa, listened to mellow jazz on the CD player, and savored the aroma of burning pine logs. She could almost forget the tension between herself and Mitch. Almost.

He sat cross-legged on the floor in front of the hearth with his back to her, coaxing the fire along, a tall glass of beer beside him. He was pure pleasure to watch. His every movement had the ease and sureness of a physically confident man, a man who kept his body honed and fit, a man accustomed to demanding peak performance from himself.

Tiffany found herself envisioning him on a ski hill.

He would be controlled yet daring, classically beautiful in form but conscious only of the pleasure of the run.

The mental picture was stirring enough to make her consider taking up the sport, until she remembered that she would be part of a crowd—a female crowd of Mitch-watchers.

"I'm starting to feel the heat," Mitch said, putting the poker back on its stand, picking up his beer, and getting to his feet.

Tiffany stared at him, beginning to think he really could read her mind, even when he wasn't looking at her. But after the first startled moment, she realized he'd meant the heat from the fire. She took a steaming sip of cocoa to squelch a giggle, nearly choking on it as Mitch began pulling his heavy sweater over his head.

Amazing, she thought. She'd seen countless bronzed male specimens on beaches in Hawaii, strutting and posturing like peacocks as they peeled off T-shirts and short-shorts to display themselves in bikini trunks, and her invariable reaction was amusement.

Yet Mitch, merely stripping down to a long-sleeved chambray shirt, made her pulse launch into a drumroll. Maybe it was because he wasn't posing. Or because he had a sense of humor. Or because he naturally radiated a virility and self-confidence that made other men seem to be trying too hard.

He draped his sweater over a footstool and sat down in the chair opposite Tiffany's, propping one ankle on the opposite knee. "Are you warm enough yet?" he asked.

"Yes, thanks," she said, intently studying the contents of her mug as she stifled another fit of nervous laughter. Was she *warm* enough? If she didn't stop simmering to a fast boil every time she looked at the man, she might have to excuse herself, slip outside, and jump into a snowbank.

That chilling prospect helped her settle down. "You said you grew up here. How did you get to be a skier in the middle of the prairies?" she asked, deciding to try some small talk.

"You're forgetting about cross-country skiing," he answered. "I do prefer downhill, though, and it's an easy matter to hop a flight to some mountain resort whenever I get the urge."

"But how did you get involved in downhill?" Tiffany persisted, glad to have a topic to pursue.

"There are a few hills around here, but I really got hooked during my teens, when Pete and I were visiting our uncle out on the West Coast. He took us to Whistler, and for me it was game over. I didn't want to do anything but hit the slopes. It was my life until—" He stopped abruptly, tipped his glass, and took a long pull at his beer.

Tiffany waited, but he didn't finish the sentence. Finally she couldn't stand it. "Until?" she prompted.

He grinned. "Until I was forced to grow up a little. Very little, some people might say." He pointed to a silver-framed photograph on the table beside Tiffany.

"I've noticed you glancing at that picture quite a few times. Yes, those two people in it are my parents. And yes, they're alive and well. Pete runs the farm because the folks have retired. They're snowbirds."

It was as heavy-handed and obvious a change of subject as Tiffany had ever experienced, but she went along with it despite her curiosity about why Mitch wouldn't want to talk about what he'd claimed was the great passion of his life. It wasn't her place to probe. Besides, she *had* been wondering about the picture, afraid to ask about the people in it in case the subject was painful. "Snowbirds?" she repeated.

"That's right. They migrate south every fall and stay there until late spring."

"So some Winnipeg natives *don't* care for its climate," Tiffany said with a so-there grin.

"Okay, some people don't," Mitch conceded. "But Mom and Dad managed to cope with it for a lot of years, and when they come back here for a few days at Christmas, they love the snow and the fresh air and the kind of fun you can only have in winter."

Tiffany gave him a dubious look, but she was intrigued, imagining the farmhouse with a decorated spruce tree in front of the bay window and swags of fragrant greenery trimming the doorways and the staircase. A deeply buried emotion swept over her, a longing she didn't want to identify.

"Why the faraway look?" Mitch asked.

Deciding he was much too perceptive, Tiffany hedged her answer. "Did I have a faraway look?"

"Very." He grinned. "Dreaming of a white Christmas?"

"Do I look like Bing Crosby?" she shot back. "Listen, my Santa comes to town on a surfboard pulled by eight tiny sea horses and a Rudolph whose nose is red from sunburn."

Mitch chuckled and shook his head. "No wonder our weather has you in a state of shock." As he spoke, a log toppled forward and rolled against the screen. He put down his glass and went back to pick up the poker and crouch in front of the hearth. "Is your family still in Hawaii?" he asked, opening the screen and deftly nudging the log back into place.

"My father's there," Tiffany answered absently, her treacherous mind dwelling on the tautness of Mitch's flanks as they strained against his jeans, the muscles rippling in his back and arms, the play of firelight on his strong features.

He turned his head and sent her a questioning glance.

"Dad's a TV executive in Honolulu," she went on hastily, shaking herself out of her reverie. "My mother's based in Maui, but she and my stepfather produce adventure travel videos, so they're usually off shooting in some exotic location."

Mitch lapsed into silence and gazed into the fire again, jabbing at the logs for no obvious purpose. "How old were you when your parents divorced?" he asked after several moments.

Tiffany arched her brows, taken aback by the blunt,

personal question. "About twelve," she answered, seeing no reason not to respond. "Why do you ask?"

"I'm still wondering about that faraway look. You seemed . . . I don't know. Wistful. Were there good Christmases before the split, awful ones afterward?"

"Not awful," she said firmly. After a moment's bittersweet recollection, she heard herself going on with unusual honesty, "But never all that great, either. Christmas was a time of lavish business entertaining, not family closeness. And Dad was always a . . . well, to put it kindly, a man who loved women. And they loved him back, so parties usually meant extra tension at home. The divorce simply put a bad marriage out of its misery. I lived with Mom, visited Dad, and eventually acquired very nice stepparents. When Dad remarried and started a second family—three little boys within just a few years—he suddenly began acting as if he'd invented fidelity and fatherhood. I love the kids, and I'm delighted that Dad rearranged his priorities, but at sixteen I wasn't mature enough to deal with the way he was suddenly dressing up in red suits and white beards and ho-ho-ho-ing all over the place. Men can be very—"

She stopped, drained her cup, and put it down on the table beside her. Getting to her feet, she folded the afghan over the back of her chair and put on her shoes to stride across the room to the bay window. Enough of this cozy scene, she decided. It was bad enough that she'd responded to a casual kiss as if she'd been marooned on an all-female planet for the past ten years. Did she have to turn Mitch into Dear Abby?

She peered through the window, scanning the road at the bottom of the property. "I hope you're right about your nephew's injury not being serious," she said as she heard Mitch replace the poker on the stand. "Isn't it taking an awfully long time for everyone to get home?"

"I know for certain that the injury wasn't serious, because when I talked to Pete he was calling from the hospital while the doctor sewed up Danny's cut," Mitch said.

Tiffany kept staring out the window, as if she could will the family to appear.

"Men can be very what, Tiffany?" Mitch asked after several moments. "What did you start to say?"

After thinking about her answer for a moment, she said simply, "Unpredictable."

"And unreliable?"

"That too."

"So can women," he said quietly. "At least, until you learn to choose predictable ones."

Tiffany wasn't sure she wanted him to elaborate, so she pretended to be enthralled by acres and acres of pristine snow crisscrossed by jagged lines of dark gray fence tops, but her whole body was taut with awareness of Mitch. What was he doing? Was he watching her? Moving across the room toward her, his stockinged feet making no sound on the thick carpet? Or was he ignoring her, not nearly as unsettled as she was?

She waited, with no idea what she was waiting for. She didn't even know why she wasn't turning around and saying something—anything, however inane. Was she hoping to feel his hands on her shoulders, gently turning her, drawing her close to him? Or for his arms to slip around her waist, pulling the full length of her against him, his lips grazing her ear, his breath fanning her skin?

Scarcely breathing, she wondered how she would react if suddenly she found him touching her, holding her, trying to entice her into sharing another kiss. She would stop him . . . wouldn't she?

The frissons of anticipation skittering through her suggested that she might not. And that thought was alarming. Hadn't she learned her lesson three years before?

Quiet sounds behind her brought her shallow breathing to a halt. Mitch's presence was like a magnetic field, moving in on her. Electrical currents seemed to enter the base of her spine, gathering force there, then thrilling through every part of her body. Her heart was pounding. Her temples throbbed.

Finally she felt his fingers lightly touching her shoulder. "Tiffany," he said softly. "Tiffany, I . . ."

She still didn't know what he was going to do or say, or how she was going to react.

And she didn't get a chance to find out.

"Speak of the devil," he said flatly.

A maroon van had turned into the long driveway up to the house. The family was home.

Tiffany almost convinced herself that she was relieved.

Having made the assumption that Danny Canfield was an only child, Tiffany was surprised when Mitch opened the front door and three youngsters—two boys and a rosy-cheeked little girl—tumbled into the house ahead of their parents.

Standing at the archway between the entrance and the living room, Tiffany smiled as she watched the happy exchange of greetings and gradually sorted out the various members of the Canfield clan.

Danny, the boy who'd been stitched up at the hospital, was the oldest. Tiffany put him at about eleven. His brother Jason was perhaps seven or eight. Both were lean but sturdy. Both had brown hair and huge, melted-chocolate eyes. After a brief, appraising survey of their father, she was sure the boys were almost exact replicas of Pete and Mitch at the same age.

She found the physical resemblance between the men striking. Pete was more heavyset than Mitch, his features less chiseled, but his eyes were the same warm brown, his hair was just as unruly, and he moved with the same easy male grace that was such a part of Mitch. Even their voices were similar. Whether they were alike in nonphysical ways remained to be seen. The obvious difference was that Pete was clearly a family man while Mitch was . . .

She couldn't finish the thought. She wasn't entirely

certain *what* Mitch was. By his own admission, he liked to keep his life as free of responsibility as possible, yet there was no question that he was close to his family, ready to give them a hand whenever he was needed, and a doting uncle. When Rebecca, a dark-eyed vixen somewhere between two and three years old, joyfully ran over to him with her arms outstretched, Mitch bent down to scoop her up and planted a noisy kiss on her cheek that made her giggle with delight. He carried her to the stairway and sat down on the steps to extricate her from her boots and snowsuit, managing the task easily, at the same time listening to the two boys excitedly relating all the gory details of Danny's mishap.

Okay, so the man's a sweet, likable rogue, Tiffany conceded. *But a rogue is a rogue is a rogue.*

What bothered her most was that she seemed so infernally concerned about what kind of man Mitch Canfield was. After all, what did it matter? The mild flirtation the two of them had toyed with didn't mean any more to her than it did to him.

Suddenly Tiffany realized that Peter Canfield was standing directly in front of her, waiting patiently for her to give him her attention. With a start, she shook hands with him and smiled her way through first-name introductions that included the children. The youngsters were polite, but not terribly interested in her. Their beloved uncle Mitch was the star of this show.

When she shared a handshake with Jackie, Tiffany was surprised to find the petite woman's grip almost as firm as her husband's. A pretty blonde with dove-gray eyes and a look of porcelain delicacy, Jackie didn't fit the stereotype of a farmer's wife and a partner in a tough business, let alone a mother of three lively youngsters.

"We're so sorry we couldn't meet you at the airport ourselves," Jackie said with an engaging smile as she gestured Tiffany toward the living room sofa. "We knew you were in good hands, though."

Very good hands, Tiffany thought, half-turning to glance back at Mitch. He shot her a wink and one of his wicked little grins, as if they shared a delicious secret. They did, of course, but she hoped he was discreet enough to let it remain a secret. She sent him a few warning daggers with her eyes until she noticed that Pete was watching with great interest. "Your farm is much bigger than I'd realized," she said brightly as she sat down beside Jackie on the sofa, crossing one leg over the other. "I'm looking forward to a tour."

Pete shooed the boys off to their basement playroom, then joined Jackie and Tiffany in the living room. As he pulled up a chair, he gave Tiffany a quick once-over, much like the one Mitch had subjected her to earlier. Yet Pete's scrutiny wasn't unsettling. There seemed to be nothing *personal* in it. Mitch's every glance seemed extremely, intimately personal. "Do you have warm clothes?" Pete asked.

"Mitch was kind enough to take me to his store and outfit me," Tiffany answered, trying not to think about the sensual moments she and Mitch had shared while he'd outfitted her.

Pete nodded. "Good. Frostbite isn't fun. I hope little brother didn't overcharge you."

Tiffany favored Mitch with an amused smile as he ambled into the living room with Rebecca riding on his shoulders. Little brother? Somehow the phrase didn't suit him. "I haven't been given a bill yet, but your little brother seems more inclined to undercharge than overcharge," she said, unable to resist the mild jibe. "I can't imagine why. I have an expense account."

"Never could resist a pretty face," Mitch said, his eyes twinkling, challenging her to another verbal duel.

"Then your store must be on the verge of bankruptcy," she retorted.

"Not really. There aren't that many faces as pretty as yours around, you know."

Tiffany felt herself turning scarlet. He'd parried her thrust masterfully, making it seem as if she'd been angling for a compliment. "You mean, the hills aren't alive with the sound of ski bunnies rustling and swishing in their wholesale snowsuits from Canfield Sports?" she said sweetly.

Mitch conceded the match with a lazy grin. "Touché, Miss Greer." He swung Rebecca down from his shoulders and carefully placed her on the floor, aiming her toward her mother.

Tiffany realized that she'd forgotten the presence of everyone in the room except Mitch. Stealing a peek at Jackie, then at Pete, she saw them exchanging bemused smiles, their eyebrows raised like question marks.

Groaning inwardly, she made up her mind to put a stop to this foolishness once and for all. With any luck, Mitch would leave soon anyway. Seriousness didn't seem to be his strong point. All she had to do was ignore him and act like the professional business-woman she was until he decided there was more fun to be had elsewhere. She would give odds that he'd be gone before dinner.

By nine o'clock, Tiffany was glad she hadn't placed any bets. She was having one of the most disconcerting evenings of her life.

Mitch hadn't left before dinner. He sat across from her at the table and made it impossible for her to ignore him during the meal. He kept drawing her into conver-sations, teasing her with tall tales about life in the north, making her laugh when what she really wanted to do was kick him under the table. And her willpower was pathetic. Whenever she thought Mitch wasn't watching, she found herself sneaking peeks at him, trying to analyze what made him so irresistible.

But he was always watching, or so it seemed. Even if he was talking to someone else, his attention not in the least focused on her, she only had to let her sidelong glance stray toward him and suddenly he was skewering her with a compelling gaze. Convinced it was all a parlor game to him, she wished she could be as blasé.

Never mind, she told herself during dessert. After dinner, when the conversation turned to distribution potentials, cash flow projections, and quality controls, Mitch would remember that he had something important to do back in town. His boredom tolerance wouldn't withstand that kind of talk.

After Rebecca and the boys had been put to bed, the adults settled into the living room for coffee. Tiffany chose one of the overstuffed armchairs opposite the sofa, preferring not to take the chance of being seated next to Mitch. He took one end of the sofa, while Jackie took the other.

Tiffany soon decided she'd have been better off in Jackie's place. Sitting directly opposite Mitch, she had to steel herself against falling under the spell of his steady, dark gaze and his easy grin. She firmly steered the idle pleasantries back to the point of her visit—the proposed share-purchase.

All at once Mitch was transformed. The ski bum suddenly turned into a combination marketing expert, financial analyst, and cross-examiner. He asked probing questions about Paradise Foods and fielded several of Tiffany's queries about Canfield Farm. "Mitch, are you part of this operation?" she finally asked, perplexed by the way Jackie and Pete seemed to defer to him. "I'm not trying to be rude," she added hastily. "It's just that you seem so . . . so involved."

"I'm family, that's all," he answered lightly. "And I've always been one to put in my two cents' worth."

"A whole lot more than two cents' worth," Pete said firmly. "Tiffany, let me explain. I'm a farmer. Mitch is the sharp businessman. He's too damn stubborn to make it official by accepting shares in the company, but he's an important part of it. His advice guides us every step of the way."

"I see," Tiffany said, nodding. So much for getting rid of Mitch with dreary shoptalk.

He shot her an innocent smile, then went on asking his incisive questions.

As she gave him her answers, she was glad she knew her stuff. She sensed that she was gaining his respect, and even though it irritated her to admit it, she wanted his respect—as a professional, of course.

What she couldn't figure out was why he'd been so determined not to have *her* respect, at least before they'd started talking business. Ski bum, indeed. "You gave me the impression that your store is successful because of a lucky fluke," she said to him at last. "There's no fluke involved. You know exactly what you're doing, and it isn't just street smarts. You've studied business administration."

"Do you have to make it sound like an accusation?" he said, laughing.

Tiffany was annoyed. Had Mitch been playing dumb, like a pool hustler letting an unsuspecting mark win a few rounds before the real action started? Did he think that kind of manipulation was necessary? Did he expect her to try to cheat his family instead of entering into honest negotiations? She narrowed her eyes and tossed another accusation at him. "You have an M.B.A., probably from a first-rate school."

Mitch sighed dramatically. "Guilty as charged."

"Why didn't you say so when I mentioned my degree? Or when we were talking about how you made a success of your business?"

"I didn't consider it relevant. Would you have felt safer with me if you'd known I had a set of letters after my name?"

"Yes," Tiffany snapped, then reversed herself. "I mean, no. Of course not."

"You mean, yes. An M.B.A. is a handy label. Labels are important to you, Ms. Greer. You think they tell you what to expect from a person, and you like to know what to expect. Spontaneity scares you."

"That's not fair," Tiffany retorted, sitting forward on her chair and gripping the edges of the cushion as if preparing to spring at him like an angry wildcat. "How can you jump to such conclusions when you hardly know me?"

Mitch grinned with maddening self-satisfaction. "Now, that reaction is very spontaneous. Maybe there's hope for you yet."

She stared at him, realizing she'd done it again. She'd forgotten that she and Mitch weren't alone in the room. She'd forgotten they weren't alone in the world!

Sliding back on the seat and folding her arms, she darted an embarrassed smile at her hosts. "Mitch and I seem to react to each other like oil and water," she said.

Mitch snorted. "Not exactly. I seem to recall—"

"Don't," she interrupted, glaring at him. "Don't you dare."

Pete cleared his throat, looked as if he was about to

say something, then cleared his throat again and left it at that.

"Anybody for more coffee?" Jackie asked, jumping up to get the carafe from the kitchen whether anyone wanted it or not.

"I'd love some," Tiffany said, getting to her feet and following Jackie. "Let me help."

Mitch held out his cup to Tiffany and smiled at her. "I'll have a refill, thanks. That is, if you don't mind getting it."

"I'd be happy to," she said, gritting her teeth in a phony smile. As she curled one hand around his cup, he brushed a fingertip over her wrist, a gesture designed to remind her of the sensual sparks between them. She jerked back her hand, almost dropping the cup as Mitch released it, but the brief contact had done its work. The tingling in her wrist sizzled along her nerve endings. She felt a phantom ache in her lips as the memory of Mitch's devastating kiss came back to haunt her. She wanted to throttle him. She wanted to throw something at him.

Unfortunately, most of all she simply wanted him.

FIVE

"I've never seen anything like it," Jackie said softly.

Pete shook his head in astonishment. "There was no warning. No yawning, no drooping eyelids, no drifting off and coming to with a start. She stopped talking right in the middle of a sentence. Do you think she's fainted?"

"She hasn't fainted," Mitch said, smiling as he watched the rhythmic rise and fall of Tiffany's breasts. He'd known for the past hour that she was running on sheer willpower. The signs had been so obvious to him, he was amazed that the others hadn't seen them. After starting out ramrod straight in her chair, she'd gradually given in to the temptation to copy Jackie, slipping out of her shoes and tucking her legs under her. He hadn't been at all surprised when her eyes ultimately closed and her head tipped sideways onto her shoulder before finding a resting spot with one cheek pressed against the back of the chair. The way she'd snuggled into the plump cushions had been causing him serious discomfort. He kept wishing he were the chair. "No wonder she couldn't stay awake," he said quietly. "The jet lag alone would be enough to knock anybody out. In the space of a few hours, Tiffany has crossed several time zones, faced arctic temperatures after knowing only the tropics all her life, socialized with new business contacts, and entered into preliminary discussions about a complicated corporate deal. We should have packed her off to bed a long time ago."

"I hate to wake her up now," Jackie murmured. "But I don't think we should leave her to sleep there."

"I could carry her upstairs and put her on the bed," Pete said as he slowly stood up. "We can pull a comforter over her."

Mitch shot to his feet. "I'll carry her," he said, his tone suggesting he wouldn't brook any argument.

Pete looked at Jackie, than back at Mitch, grinning. "What's with you, anyway? You act as if you have some kind of claim on the lady. That's not like you, Mitch. Not at all."

"Don't make a big thing of it," Mitch said with a scowl. "It's just that I think that if Tiffany happened to wake up, she'd be more embarrassed to find herself in your arms than in mine. Being carried, I mean."

"I knew what you meant," Pete said, one brow raised. "Is there any special reason why she'd feel less embarrassed in your arms?"

"Don't give Mitch a hard time," Jackie ordered.

"I'm sure he's right." She turned to spear Mitch with a threatening look. "But if you think I'm going to let you undress her and tuck her in . . ."

"Don't worry," Mitch said, relaxing into a grin. "I'm going to be a perfect gentleman if it kills me. She's too young and innocent for my taste." He bent down to slide his arms under Tiffany's slender body. "She's really out of it," he said, lifting her as he straightened up. He hoped he was right. She'd be mortified if she woke up.

His heart was pounding out a syncopated rhythm by the time he reached the bedroom, and not because Tiffany was a healthy armful to carry up a flight of stairs. She was also an extremely sexy armful. Sleep had made her soft and pliant as she settled against him, burrowing her face into his neck, her lips almost touching the hollow of his throat and her warm breath tickling his skin. He didn't want to put her down, pull a comforter over her, and leave. He wanted to close the bedroom door behind them both, gently liberate her from her clothes, and crawl into bed with her.

There was nothing unusual about that reaction, Mitch reflected. What *was* unusual, what shocked him, was that he simply wanted to hold her, to feel her skin against his skin, her legs tangled with his legs, her breasts molded to his chest. If nothing else happened, cuddling her all night long would be a profound pleasure in itself.

He wondered if he should check his I.D.

Or maybe a hovering spacecraft had sucked out his

brain before he'd entered the airport terminal earlier in the day.

Lowering Tiffany to the mattress, Mitch looked down at her and felt something stirring inside him. Something deeply disturbing. He tried to tell himself he was experiencing only a normal response to hair the color of a midnight sky, to thick fringes of sooty lashes lying against creamy, delicate skin, to cheekbones a sculptor would want to immortalize in marble.

But he knew he was kidding himself. What he was feeling had nothing to do with the shape of a cheekbone or the inky shade of a lock of hair. He even suspected it had precious little to do with raw desire. This innocent-looking woman was bewitching him. If he had any sense, he would make tracks fast.

Yet he lingered, covering her with the quilt and smoothing silky tendrils of her hair back from her face as he tried to decipher what it was about Tiffany Greer that struck such a responsive chord in him.

Instead of finding an answer, he felt a wave of tenderness sweeping over him, as powerful as it was incomprehensible. Hardly aware of what he was doing, he leaned down and lightly kissed her eyelids, then reluctantly started to pull away.

Her eyes flew open. She stared at him so intently, he wondered if she was disoriented or confused or even frightened.

Mitch opened his mouth to reassure her and explain what had happened, but before he could speak, Tiffany's lips curved in a sweet, drowsy smile. "Hi, Mitch," she murmured, as if she'd known and trusted him forever. Reaching for his hand, she sighed contentedly and went back to sleep.

Time stopped as Mitch stared down at her, a lump rising in his throat. After an eternity he blinked and gave himself a mental shake. A lump in Mitch Canfield's throat? Because of a woman? A woman he'd met that day? A too-young, too-innocent woman who belonged in the South Seas and shouldn't even try to stay in this raw, rough country? What the hell was happening?

He carefully extricated his hand and stood up. After gazing down at Tiffany for several more moments, he slowly backed out of the room. When he reached the door, he took a deep breath and forced himself to leave.

If there was one thing he'd learned over the past few years, it was when to make a quick and definite exit.

It might be a good idea, he decided, to give the farm a wide berth for a little while.

Mitch knocked the receiver from his bedside phone onto the night table, coming awake slowly and fighting every step of the way as the shrill ringing dragged him from Tiffany's embrace.

"Uncle Mitch?" he heard.

Clumsily retrieving the receiver, Mitch glanced at his alarm clock. Six-thirty. His nephews were true farm boys, with their chores undoubtedly finished already. "Danny? Is anything wrong?" he asked, shaking enough lingering sensual images from his brain to leave room for worry.

"Kinda," Danny said. "Remember when you took me to the library on Saturday to work on my science project?"

Rubbing his eyes with his thumb and forefinger, Mitch grunted in the affirmative.

"Well, I can't find the notes I made," Danny said. "I've looked all over, and I need them at school today. I was wondering if maybe I left my notebook at your place when we went back there for pizza."

"Hang on. I'll go take a look around," Mitch said, putting the receiver down on his pillow and swinging his legs over the side of the bed. He sat on the edge of the mattress for a moment, then pushed himself to his feet and headed for the living room. A glimpse of his naked body in the full-length standing mirror confirmed what he already knew. He'd ended the previous day with an urgent desire for Tiffany Greer, and he was starting the new day in the same uncomfortable condition.

He also looked as if he'd had a bad night. His hair was sticking up every which way, he needed a shave badly, and there were circles under his eyes. He'd spent the first part of the night battling a frustrating bout of insomnia and the remainder whirling in a kaleidoscope of erotic dreams.

It took him a few minutes to find Danny's book. He shook his head as he picked up the phone in the living room. "Danny, why is it that your memory is so sharp you could pinpoint the exact location of your book, but you're so absentminded you keep leaving your things here in the first place?"

"That's what Mom asked," Danny said. "I think maybe the problem is that I always have such a good time with you, I forget about everything else."

Mitch snorted. He obviously wasn't the only Canfield who'd mastered the art of the snow job.

Suddenly a mental picture of Tiffany's laughing face forced its way to the forefront of his mind, the way it had in all his dreams: Tiffany in his old bedroom, her eyes sparkling with humor as he babbled that nonsense about snowflowers; Tiffany in his arms, smiling up at him; Tiffany lying on the bed—*his* bed . . . "Nice try, kid," he said hastily, dragging his attention back to Danny. "So what do we do now?"

"Well, I suppose I could explain to the teacher. She'd probably only dock me ten marks or so."

"Bring on the violins," Mitch said, unable to keep the amusement out of his voice. "Okay, buddy. I'm on my way."

"Hey, thanks," Danny said, managing to sound surprised.

"You're welcome. But next time you're here I'm going to attach your belongings to you. These early-morning runs are getting to be too much for a decrepit old man like me."

"I know, Uncle Mitch. I'm really sorry. Honest."

Mitch scowled at the receiver. He hadn't meant for the boy to *agree* that he was decrepit. "I'll be there before the school bus rolls around," he promised. "That's at eight, right?"

"Right. I owe you one for this, Uncle Mitch."

Mitch rolled his eyes as he hung up.

He was halfway through his shower before he remembered that he hadn't planned to go near the farm while Tiffany was there. But it shouldn't be a problem, he told himself. She wouldn't be up anyway.

Tiffany woke to the sounds of a household in which it was obvious that everyone was trying in vain to be quiet while going about normal morning routines.

She groped for the travel clock she'd put on her bedside table in the middle of the night. It had been after three when she'd opened her eyes and slowly figured out where she was and who had put her there. She'd barely managed to keep from groaning out loud. After changing to her nightgown and unpacking her bags, she'd gone back to bed only to lie awake and stare at the ceiling, compulsively going over and over every detail of every conversation with Mitch, reliving each touch and the single, sweet kiss they'd shared.

She brought the alarm clock close to her face and peered at it. Seven o'clock. She put the clock back and snuggled down under the covers, hugging her pillow.

Ten minutes later, Tiffany accepted the fact that she wasn't going to go back to sleep. Her mind kept struggling to capture the vague memory of Mitch carrying her up to bed, bending over her, his eyes filled with a curious warmth, his hand gently stroking her hair. She'd been struck by an uncanny sense of closeness that still refused to be shaken off. The cold light of dawn was supposed to bring a person to her senses, she mused. Why wasn't it working?

Abruptly, she decided to get up. No formal plans had been made for working with Pete and Jackie on the first morning after her journey, but there didn't seem to be much point lying around dwelling on the strange events of the previous day. Besides, the sooner she faced her hosts, the sooner it would be over. She couldn't imagine what they must think of her, not only for her Sleeping Beauty act but for her heated exchanges with Mitch.

The one thing that made her embarrassment bearable was that she wouldn't have to face Mitch. Perhaps by the time he did show up at the farm again, she would be the sane, sensible woman who'd left Hawaii a little more than a day ago. She might even be impervious to the man's sensual impact by then. Her wild response to him *must* have been caused by jet lag. She'd read that it could do weird things to a person.

The kitchen was as big and cheerful and cozy as Tiffany had always felt a farmhouse kitchen should be, all bleached oak with blue trim, sprigged wallpaper, and bright curtains. The boys were outside roughhousing in the snow while waiting for the school bus, Pete was shoveling the driveway, and Rebecca was under the long oval kitchen table, crawling around in her fuzzy pink pajamas as she played her own private, happy games.

It was a homey scene that Tiffany was enjoying thoroughly. Dressed in a bright green jogging suit and white canvas loafers, she sat at the end of the table savoring a mug of steaming coffee along with fresh-baked biscuits and a plate of fresh fruit. She watched, fascinated, as Jackie handled countless chores and minor crises with a minimum of fuss and a maximum of efficiency while not missing a beat in their chat.

Tiffany's apology had been offered and laughingly brushed aside. "Mitch was right," Jackie had said. "After that long flight and the time zones you'd crossed, we shouldn't have kept you up as long as we did."

Tiffany couldn't help wondering whether Mitch had made excuses for her before he'd put her to bed or afterward. Not that it made any difference, but she was rankled by the knowledge that while she'd snoozed with the childlike innocence more suited to Rebecca than to a grown woman, he'd taken it upon himself to decide what to do about her. Her one consolation was that he hadn't seen fit to get her into her nightgown.

She banished that thought as a treacherous warmth started curling through her. "Jackie, can't I help with something?" she asked brightly.

Jackie smiled. "No thanks. Everything's under control. Relax. You'll be working like a demon soon enough. There's a lot of ground to cover in the next few days, if you're going to get a really good look at what our operation's all about."

Tiffany felt a sudden stream of cold air swirling around her bare ankles. She looked over at the house's back entrance.

After a vigorous stamping of feet, Pete poked his head into the kitchen. "Honey, is there another container of lock deicer in the cupboard under the sink?" he asked Jackie. "The truck door won't budge."

Lock deicers, Tiffany thought as Pete took the canister Jackie handed him and went back outside. Driveways and footpaths that needed shoveling because the wind had redistributed the snowdrifts during the night. Stamping on the doormat to knock snow off boots every time someone came in from outside. Bundling up from head to toe whenever anyone went out. Did she really want to let herself in for all that for more than a few days?

She had no choice, she reminded herself. If a deal was struck, she might have to stay whether she liked it or not.

A few minutes later, Pete poked his head in again, holding out the canister. "That worked, so I'll be on my way as soon as the engine's warmed up." He glanced at Tiffany and gave her a grin that made her insides clench because it was so like Mitch's amused little smile. "I don't know why I'm rushing," he said. "I'm going to the dentist."

Tiffany laughed and clucked her tongue sympathetically, but abruptly looked away when Jackie went to the door to give Pete a kiss. Their easy affection some-how got to her.

Pete had been gone for about five minutes, Rebecca had scooted out to the living room, and Jackie had hurried after her when Tiffany felt another draft on her ankles and heard another round of foot-stamping. She wondered if Pete's truck had stalled because he hadn't let the engine run long enough. She looked up, brows raised questioningly.

But it wasn't Pete who appeared in the doorway this time. It was Mitch, one hand pulling off his cap and shoving it into his pocket while the other unzipped his jacket. His eyes met Tiffany's and widened. He looked completely taken aback as he stopped dead in the middle of the short staircase. "What are you doing here?" he demanded.

SIX

Tiffany was shaken, the breath knocked out of her. How could any man look so appealing with his hair all mussed from his cap, and his forehead creased in a startled frown? How could he look so sexy and touchable when his lean body was encased in so many layers of clothing? It was all she could do to pretend to be unaffected. She shifted her gaze from one side to the other, as if checking to see precisely where she was and why he should be surprised to find her there. "Um . . . You brought me here, remember?"

"I know that," he said impatiently. "But what are you doing in the kitchen?"

She looked down at her plate, then back at him. "Eating breakfast?"

Exasperated, he tried once more. "I mean, why are you up so early? You should be catching up on some rest."

"I couldn't sleep," she answered.

"You were doing pretty well the last time I saw you."

Tiffany didn't think it was necessary for him to remind her of her fall from grace, but she decided her manners would be impeccable even if his weren't. There would be no repeat of the foolish bickering of the night before. "I woke up," she explained pleasantly. "I guess I'm still on Hawaii time, or at least somewhere in the middle of the Pacific." No need to tell him *he* was the cause of her sleeplessness. "By the way, thanks for the lift—literally," she forced herself to add.

She was rewarded by a hint of a smile. "As always, my pleasure," he murmured, then propped one foot on the top step and leaned down to unlace his boot.

It occurred to Tiffany that Mitch didn't seem as happy-go-lucky or flirtatious as he'd been the day before. And he looked as if his night hadn't been any more restful than hers. Had he spent it with some willing woman?

Jackie rescued her from that oddly upsetting thought by breezing back into the kitchen with Rebecca in her arms. "Mitch, you're spoiling my son," she scolded as she went to the door to greet him. "How is Danny going to learn to be responsible for his own things if you keep returning them? I told him not to ask you to drive out here this morning."

"He didn't," Mitch said, taking off his boot and switching his position to unlace the other one. "Danny only asked whether his notebook was at my place. He even offered to take his lumps with the teacher. It was my choice to rescue him one more time. After all, I knew he'd had the book with him at my place, and I didn't remember it when we left, so how can I be tough on him for forgetting?" When both boots were off, he straightened up, took off his jacket, and tossed it onto a hook, then padded into the kitchen in thick gray work socks.

He was wearing a black turtleneck shell under a multicolored Nordic pullover. Black stretch pants hugged the lines of his lean hips and thighs.

Steady, Tiffany told herself desperately as her breathing grew erratic and her hands began trembling.

"Anyway," he went on without another glance at her, "I made it here just before the bus arrived to pick up the kids for school, so I think our boy was nervous enough to decide to be more careful next time." His face lit up with a grin as Rebecca held out her arms to him. "How's my Becky?" he said, taking the child and tossing her high enough over his head to make her squeal delightedly.

Tiffany tried not to watch the scene. It did inexplicable things to her insides. But she couldn't look away.

"Give her back to me," Jackie ordered with an indulgent smile. "Now that the rest of the family's taken care of, it's time to get this one dressed."

Mitch surrendered the little girl and went over to the stove. Lifting a lid, he peered into the pot. "Has everyone eaten?"

"There's plenty of porridge left for you," Jackie said. "I had an inkling that Danny might have conned you into showing up, so I made extra. Help yourself."

As Jackie took Rebecca upstairs and Mitch proceeded to get a bowl from the cupboard without even trying to make conversation, Tiffany began to feel distinctly ignored. Fine, she thought. She didn't want to talk to the man anyway. She concentrated on finishing the last of her fruit plate and a few remaining morsels of honeyed biscuit.

Mitch was ladling porridge into his bowl when, without looking back at her, he said, "Tiffany, I know you have socks because I picked them out myself. You shouldn't go around with bare ankles. There are cold drafts at floor level, especially where you're sitting."

She looked up at him with a start. He'd noticed her ankles? She felt a renewal of warmth flickering inside her, but quelled it rapidly and decisively. All he'd noticed was something he could nag her about. With another pasted-on smile, she said sweetly, "It's so nice to see you again, Mitch, though I'm not sure I can handle your overwhelming charm so early in the morning."

Mitch turned his head to shoot Tiffany a sharp glance, but grinned as he realized he deserved her ironic remark. He'd been so wrapped up in trying not to reveal how bowled over he was at seeing her, he'd been brusque to the point of rudeness.

As he took his filled bowl to the counter and drizzled a bit of maple syrup over the oatmeal, he forced a silent confession from himself. During the drive to the farm, hadn't he been hoping Tiffany would be up? In fact, hadn't he suspected that the time change would have her wide awake no matter how tired she was? The shock waves that had rippled through him when he'd walked into the house and looked into those bottomless sea-green eyes of hers had been triggered by the intensity of his pleasure at seeing her, not by genuine surprise.

He moved to the table to sit down at the far end from Tiffany, wondering why he couldn't shake off his feelings for her. Of course, it didn't help that she looked fresh and wholesome without a bit of makeup on and slightly damp curls framing her face, her slender curves all too obvious under her jogging suit, her lips soft and kissable. Why couldn't she have been the type who needed cosmetics and a perfect hairdo to look good? Or was he in real trouble? Would this woman seem gorgeous to him no matter how she looked to the rest of the world?

Maybe his emotions were in a knot because of the way she'd lit up for an unguarded instant when she'd seen him. There had been times when he'd watched with reluctant envy as that same glowing expression appeared in Jackie's eyes when she saw Pete. It was enough to make a man feel like every hero who ever lived.

That was it, Mitch decided. That was the key to what was happening. It was nothing serious after all. Tiffany was good for his ego. He could deal with that weakness. "What did you have for breakfast?" he asked.

Tiffany, lifting her cup to her lips, frowned over the rim. All of a sudden the man wanted to be sociable. "Jackie made up a fruit plate for me," she answered.

"A fruit plate. That's a Hawaiian breakfast, not a Winnipeg breakfast."

"It's my kind of breakfast," Tiffany said firmly. "Jackie assumed that a light meal of fresh fruit is what I'm used to, and she assumed right."

"Maybe it's what you're used to, but around here you'd be better off with porridge. Jackie makes it tastier than most. Grates a bit of nutmeg into it, maybe some cinnamon. In any case, it's the kind of fuel you need in this country. Sticks to your ribs and heats your insides."

"I'm not into rib-sticking food, and I certainly don't need my—" She clamped her mouth shut, realizing that she'd almost admitted that the last thing she needed was to have her insides heated. Mitch's presence was enough to do that job more than adequately no matter how annoying he was, but she certainly didn't want to admit it to him.

It was too late, she realized as she saw him watching her, his spoon suspended halfway to his mouth, the familiar knowing grin tugging at one corner of his lips.

"Don't you have to get back to town to open your store?" she asked pointedly.

He laughed and shot her a look of utter horror. "Are you serious? Do you honestly think I'd *work* in that place? What's the point of being the boss if you're not going to hire people to do the day-to-day drudgery?"

Tiffany studied him, her eyes narrowing. "I'm not buying your ski-bum act anymore," she said firmly. "Nobody makes a success of a competitive business with the attitude you try to project. Why do you do that?"

"Do what?"

"Pretend to be something you're not."

He looked her straight in the eye. "On the contrary. I'm one of the few people I know who *doesn't* pretend to be something I'm not. What you see is what you get. There's nothing more, nothing hidden, nothing profound under the veneer. Don't endow me with qualities I don't possess, Tiffany. That's a woman's greatest weakness and worst habit. She insists on seeing a man as being better than he is, then hates him when he doesn't measure up to her image of him."

Tiffany gaped at him, astonished by the vehemence of his lecture. He'd spoken in his usual lazy drawl, with his usual wise-guy smile, but his words told their own story and a sudden hardness in his eyes confirmed it. "What's this?" she asked softly when she'd recovered some of her poise. "Are you giving me fair warning, Mitch?"

Putting down his spoon, Mitch silently cursed himself. What the hell had prompted that speech? He'd sounded like a cynical egotist, cautioning a gorgeous woman not to get herself all wrapped up in him. As if he

was such a prize. Well, he was no prize, and he probably *was* a cynical egotist. And maybe Tiffany was too
soft and sweet for her own good. She needed to be
warned about men like Mitch Canfield. They wouldn't
all be so careful not to take advantage of her.

He stood up, strode to the other end of the table,
curved his hands around her shoulders, and lifted her to
her feet. "Yeah," he said, his voice suddenly husky.
"Fair warning for both of us." He lowered his mouth to
hers in a kiss that was all demand, no finesse. He meant
it to be that way. He didn't want to indulge in gentle,
coaxing nibbles designed to entice a woman into wanting more. This was a final kiss. An end to the craziness.

At first, Tiffany was too astonished to protest. After
only a few seconds, she was too involved, too lost in
pleasure to offer even token resistance.

Mitch's tongue, hot and aggressive, parted her lips
and delved into the recesses behind them. She tasted
the spicy bouquet of nutmeg, cinnamon, and sugary
maple as her own tongue instinctively met and stroked
his.

When his hands left her shoulders and plowed into
her hair, tilting her head back as he deepened his
possession of her mouth, her arms snaked around his
waist and tightened, pulling his body against hers. She
heard a low, sensual growl rumbling in his throat and
felt its vibrations against her lips. She was acutely aware
of the tautness of him pressing into her, and a heavy,
delicious ache settled between her thighs. She'd never

known she could experience such an instant, mindless need.

He brought one of his hands down to rest along the side of her jaw as his kiss gentled, his tongue stroking her lips as if to soothe them after the rough onslaught of his mouth. Tiffany moaned with pleasure, and Mitch slowly feathered his fingertips along the column of her throat, then let his palm glide downward until it cupped her breast.

She caught her breath and strained against his hand, at the same time pushing her hands up under his sweater, then under his cotton shell to explore the contours of his back and feel the warmed silk of his skin.

Following her lead, he slid his hand under her jersey, rested it on her bare midriff for a long, tantalizing moment, brushing his thumb back and forth over the underside of one of her breasts, then teased the nipple until it was a swollen nub of concentrated desire.

He released her mouth and dragged his lips over her throat while he disentangled his hand from her hair and brought it down to her other breast, subjecting its sensitive tip to his special brand of erotic torment. As her back arched, he gently kneaded and shaped the high, firm mounds.

Tiffany was floating in a state of blissful abandon. Her hands moved constantly over Mitch's back and sides, ventured to his chest and shoulders, rubbed lightly over his hard male nipples. She loved the feel of him. The heat, the textures, the harnessed strength she sensed in every movement of the muscles under his skin, the scratchiness of the V-shaped pelt that narrowed to a thin line at his waist.

Mitch groaned again as her tongue stroked his and lured it into a tantalizing dance. "You're driving me right out of my mind," he whispered. "This isn't what was supposed to happen, Tiffany. This isn't the way I'd scripted it. You turn all my intentions inside out. You defeat me at every turn without even trying, without knowing what you're doing to me." He caught her full lower lip between his teeth and nibbled gently on it, then drew his tongue across it soothingly. "I don't understand any of this," he said as his lips closed once again over hers.

Tiffany didn't understand any of it, either. But she didn't care. The room was whirling. The floor was tilting up and down like a raft on choppy waters, and she was clinging to Mitch, her equilibrium distorted and her legs too weak to support her.

As if he knew how shaky she was, he slid both hands down her body until they cupped her bottom, then lifted her so she was sitting on the edge of the table. Moving between her thighs, he dug his fingers into her soft flesh to press her against him.

"Mitch," she whispered against his mouth. "Oh, Mitch, why do I want you so much? How can I want a man I don't even know?"

The naïveté of her question brought Mitch to his senses faster than a shovelful of snow hurled in his face. He raised his head and gazed down at her, searching

her glazed eyes, berating himself for starting something he shouldn't finish. Tiffany wasn't fair game.
Not for him. The women in his life wouldn't ask such a
thing. They didn't need to know a man to want him.
Hell, they preferred not to know too much. No intimacy, no promises, no strings. Safe sex emotionally as
well as physically. It was all a little too cold-blooded
and false for his taste, but Tiffany was a little too
warm-blooded and real for his peace of mind.

Cradling her face between his hands, he forced
himself to smile down at her, hoping he was managing
his most insolent, arrogant grin. "Maybe if you knew
me, you *wouldn't* want me so much," he suggested
quietly, though as soon as he'd spoken he wished he'd
thought twice before opening his mouth. That kind of
comment was on a level with a cheap "you're too good
for me" line that played to a woman's curiosity and
compassion.

Tiffany emerged slowly from a fog of sensuality,
her body on fire while her mind tried to come to grips
with the abrupt fading of Mitch's passion. "What did
you say?" she asked.

Mitch shook his head. "Nothing."

"But . . ."

"Nothing worth repeating," he said firmly. Realizing he'd broken the spell but not the clinch, he took
hold of Tiffany's hands and stepped back, tugging just
enough to get her to hop down from the table. At a loss
about how to smooth over the awkward moment, he

simply released her, briefly ruffled her hair as if she were a cute puppy, and started clearing the table.

Tiffany went back to her chair in a daze.

"How do things look to you so far?" he asked, acting as though nothing exceptional had happened between them and idle chitchat was perfectly natural.

"What things?" Tiffany asked in a tiny, strained voice.

"Winnipeg things. Winter things." Mitch stacked his empty bowl with her plate and carried them to the sink. "Will you be able to hack the northern life if you strike a deal with Pete and Jackie and find yourself stationed here for a while?"

She lifted her shoulders in a little shrug. "I'm not sure," she said, adding silently that there was a lot she wasn't sure about. The games Mitch played, for instance. "I'm just not sure," she repeated, more to herself than to him.

"Yet you still think you can be objective about your recommendation?"

"Yes," she said, her chin shooting up as she snapped out of her trance and started helping with the cleanup. Enough of this starry-eyed silliness, she told herself. "If the two companies are right for each other, I'll have no trouble recommending a share-purchase. Anyway, Paradise Foods isn't likely to back out of the deal if I decide I'm not prepared to stay for the transition period. It's a very large corporation, with holdings all over the world. There's bound to be some eccentric soul somewhere who'd love to come here."

"I see," Mitch said as he washed the dishes, mulling over her words. She might leave Winnipeg. He might never see her again. Maybe it would be just as well, but he didn't like the idea. "Eccentric?" he repeated, fastening on the telling word. "That bad, huh?"

Tiffany grabbed a dishtowel and started drying. "Mitch, I got here only yesterday," she pointed out. "I admit I'm a bit overwhelmed by the toughness that seems to be necessary to get along here, but I'm not ready to back down from the challenge before I've given myself a chance to meet it."

He shot her a sidelong glance and a grin. "Honey, you might as well cry uncle now. You're not that kind of tough. You'd be a fragile orchid trying to survive on a sheet of ice."

"Oh really?" Her chin went up again as she favored him with a cool smile. "How do you know I'm not a hardy snowflower?"

Mitch laughed. "Care to place any bets?"

"On what? My ability to make adjustments to an unfamiliar environment?" Setting aside her own doubts, Tiffany decided she'd had enough of being condescended to because she hadn't been born and raised in a snowbank. "I'll take your bet," she said defiantly. "What are the stakes?"

Mitch stalled for time by draining the sink and wiping down the counter. He hadn't expected Tiffany's response, but he realized he should have known her pride would get into the act. Now she would endure anything the north could dish out rather than admit she couldn't take it. And he'd backed himself into a corner. Now he was going to have to prove that winter in Winnipeg could defeat her—but he couldn't make up his mind whether he wanted to win the bet or lose it.

"Well?" Tiffany prompted as she put the last dish away and hung up the towel. "Are you going to name your stakes?"

It occurred to Mitch that he could make Tiffany back down from this foolishness before it started. "Okay, how about this?" he said, grabbing a hand towel to dry off with as he turned to her, trying to look sincere. "The way I figure it, you'll have to spend at least ten days here to do a comprehensive report."

Tiffany folded her arms across her midriff in an instinctively self-protective gesture. There was a dangerous gleam in Mitch's eyes. What was she getting herself into now? "Probably more like two or three weeks."

"Let's say two weeks, then. If you can last that long without admitting you could never hang in here for the long run, I'll fly you to some idyllic Caribbean hideaway for a weekend."

"A weekend in the Caribbean?" she murmured, understanding what the gleam was all about. "Sounds wonderful," she said calmly, then beamed her brightest smile at him. "And if I lose, you go with me?"

Mitch stared at her for a moment before chuckling appreciatively. It had been a long time since he'd been put in his place, and never quite so deftly. "So we're on?" he asked, thrusting out his hand.

Tiffany accepted the handshake. It was firm and warm and sizzling with electricity, but she ignored the warning buzzes and concentrated on how she was going to show this smug male what she was made of. "I am if you are," she answered.

Their gazes met and locked, their smiles gradually fading, their hands remaining clasped until several moments later when they heard Jackie and Rebecca coming down the stairs, singing a nonsense song. A loud, here-we-come nonsense song.

Tiffany shoved her hands into her pockets as Jackie and her daughter entered the kitchen. The little girl ran straight for her uncle, and he obligingly put her up on his shoulders. "What are the plans for this morning?" he asked Jackie.

"We didn't have any plans. We didn't expect a person who'd traveled halfway around the world to be raring to go so early." Jackie paused for a moment, then shook her head. "You'd probably like to get the grand tour out of the way and put yourself ahead of schedule, Tiffany, but Becky's sitter won't be here until one o'clock, so I can't show you around."

"That's okay," Tiffany said. "I'll just go for a walk."

"You might want to reconsider that idea," Mitch put in, then winced as Rebecca grabbed a clump of his hair so she could hang on while she bounced up and down in a determined attempt to get him to play giddyap. "It's twenty-five below out there. And today's windchill factor is forty below."

Tiffany knew he was trying to alarm her—and he was succeeding. "What is this windchill factor thing?"

Doing an odd little gallop in circles while Rebecca giggled happily, Mitch explained in the simplest terms possible. "The thermometer registers twenty-five below, but the wind on your skin makes it seem much colder." He paused to grin at Tiffany. "There's good news, though. The high today is supposed to reach twenty below," he went on. "Maybe even eighteen."

She smiled as if encouraged. "Well, then, it'll be practically balmy, so I believe I will go for that walk. If you'll all excuse me, I'll dash upstairs and start piling on my specially selected survival gear."

Turning on her heel and heading toward the main hall and the stairway, Tiffany heard Mitch chuckling. "Don't forget your underwear," he said as she reached the door.

She stopped and whirled on him. "Mitch! For heaven's sake, must you be so . . ." Stopping abruptly as she saw Jackie making a futile effort to suppress a bubble of laughter, Tiffany took a deep breath, let it out on a count of five, and smiled. "He means thermal underwear," she explained.

"I . . . I assumed that," Jackie said, her voice strained.

Tiffany felt a fierce blush sweeping over her. Gritting her teeth, she turned and marched out of the room.

"Make it snappy and I'll give you the tour," Mitch called after her.

"I'll take my time and wait for Jackie to give it to me this afternoon, thank you," she said, hurrying up the stairs. "You seem to be dressed for skiing. Don't change your plans on my account."

Mitch appeared in the hallway below, Rebecca still riding him like a Triple Crown jockey. "I don't blame you for begging off, of course. Since I do happen to be dressed for skiing, I'd want to head across the fields in a snowmobile. A tour would be faster that way, but those machines can be pretty scary to somebody who isn't used to them."

Reaching the first landing of the stairway, Tiffany leaned over the banister and glared down at him. "Snowmobiles do not scare me, understand? And neither do you!"

"Good. Then get a move on, and we'll be through that tour before you can say Warm and Wonderful Waikiki." He turned and went back into the kitchen, leaving Tiffany to marvel at how neatly he'd pulled off that maneuver.

What she wondered was why.

She was back in the kitchen within fifteen minutes, silky underwear caressing her skin, warm socks on her feet, ski pants swishing with every step she took.

SEVEN

A snowmobile, Tiffany decided, was like a giant, bucking mosquito on skis, assaulting her eardrums with its strident whine as it whisked her on its back across the open fields.

But it wasn't the cacaphony or the breakneck speed of the ride that kept her on edge, or the bracing cold, or the blinding glare of the sun on the endless expanse of white. She was outfitted for a polar expedition, complete with shaded goggles pulled on over her ski mask. Her own opinion was that she could pass for the mosquito's firstborn, but that seemed to be the accepted look for braving the elements.

What was keeping her nerves taut and her thoughts distracted was the way she was perched behind Mitch, her legs as well as her arms wrapped around him, her inner thighs gripping his hips. All the layers of clothing between them didn't lessen the unsettling intimacy of the position, and the constant vibration and slight shifting of their bodies heightened sensations she didn't want to feel at all. There wasn't much room to maneuver, either, with two pairs of snowshoes strapped to the sides of the machine. "Why do we need snowshoes?" she'd asked when they'd left the farmhouse.

"Insurance," Mitch had answered. "If the machine conks out, we walk. And trying to walk across a field of deep snow is like trying to walk across an unfrozen lake. You sink."

She was sinking, all right. Sinking into a state of urgent desire.

She couldn't help wondering if holding on so tightly was really necessary. It seemed to her that resting her hands on Mitch's waist and maintaining a couple of inches of space in front of her should keep her from falling off, but Mitch had insisted that she hunker up close, biker style.

As they approached their first destination, the roar of the motor eased off. The vehicle and its caterwauling stopped completely when Mitch pulled up beside a shoveled, packed path leading to a weathered old building. "A windmill," Tiffany said with a sudden smile. "Is this where the cereals are made and the flours stone-ground?"

"That's right," Mitch answered. "The old-fashioned way, now considered new-fashioned because it's environmentally friendly. Pete works this farm using techniques passed down for generations. He likes to say he was so far behind the times he ended up ahead of them, but that's just his dumb-farm-boy act."

"So you both misrepresent yourselves," Tiffany commented. "Pete plays dumb farm boy when he's really a sophisticated agricultural businessman. You try to come across as a carefree flake when you're actually a—"

"You can let go now," Mitch cut in, glancing over his shoulder at Tiffany with a grin.

She hastily pulled her arms from around his waist and reached up to yank off her mask as she shook her head to liven up her flattened hair. He'd managed to fluster her again, and just when she was trying to put *him* on the defensive. It was impossible to get the best of the man!

Mitch climbed off the machine and turned to extend a helping hand to her. Tiffany accepted it. She'd learned that lesson at the airport.

He was still holding her hand when they entered a small porch just inside the building. "You can let go now," she said, smiling sweetly up at him.

He did release her, but only to curl one arm around her middle and pull her against him. "You're a brat," he said, his mouth perilously close to hers. "Remind me not to give you a shot unless I want it to ricochet back at me."

"That's exactly what I've been trying to remind you," she said as she looked around nervously. The porch was closed off from the interior of the building by an inner door, so nobody could see what was going on. But someone could come out any minute. "I'd also like you to remember that I'm here in a professional capacity," she added. "Would you please treat me accordingly?" She ordered her pulse to settle down. It ignored her, bolting and galloping like a runaway racehorse. She squared her shoulders. "Shall we go in now?"

Mitch smiled down at her for a long moment, a thoughtful expression in his eyes. Finally releasing her, he reached out to open the door. "After you," he said with a courtly bow.

Inside the mill, Mitch turned into a different person, as he had during the business session the night before. After taking Tiffany's jacket and hanging it up, he showed her around the building, introduced her to the workers, and patiently explained everything they were doing. He was knowledgeable, serious, and unfailingly courteous.

Tiffany noticed that everyone knew him and called him by his first name, which didn't surprise her. But she was bemused by the fact that they all seemed to find it perfectly normal that he was showing her around as if he ran the place.

"Are you *sure* you're not part of this company?" she asked as they donned their jackets to go on to their next stop.

"Just family," he said. "I believe in what Pete and Jackie are doing to keep the old homestead thriving in changing times, that's all."

"Are you against a joint venture with Paradise Foods?"

"On the contrary, I'm the one who suggested it." Noticing that Tiffany was struggling to get the bottom teeth of her jacket zipper meshed properly, Mitch took over. "As long as you negotiate in good faith and don't try to change the rules about the property itself being excluded from the deal, I'll be happy."

"We're interested in the products coming out of this operation, not in the land or buildings," Tiffany assured him, adding stiffly, "And I negotiate in good faith or I don't negotiate at all."

He pulled up her zipper, then chucked her under the chin. "There goes that fighting chin again," he said. "Up and out, right on cue."

Tiffany scowled, deciding that Mitch was too adept at getting whatever reaction he liked from her just to amuse himself. Hiding behind a mask might even the odds a bit.

He watched her drag the thing over her head and face, then shook his head and laughed. "I have news for you, by the way," he said, unexpectedly drawing her into his arms. "Tiffany Greer would never make it as a terrorist or a bank robber."

Her heartbeat accelerated. "Why not?"

"Because your eyes are too beautiful and your mouth is too soft," he murmured, lowering his lips to hers. "*America's Most Wanted* is a definite possibility, though." His kiss was achingly gentle. Seductive. Persuasive.

It was the strangest feeling, Tiffany thought, to have most of her face covered while her mouth was being explored with such leisurely attention. Sensation seemed concentrated there, and she was experiencing an inexplicable, heady sense of freedom. Behind the mask, she could be anyone, even an uninhibited, fearless woman who took her pleasure where she found it, who hadn't been made wary by the past, who asked no questions of the future.

But Mitch remembered where they were and who they were. "We'd better push on before we do something that'll be the scandal of Canfield Farm," he said, releasing her.

Tiffany sighed. He was right, of course. But she wished he would think about the consequences of his sensual teasing *before* he indulged in it. One of these times he was liable to find himself flat on his back in the snow, and to hell with the scandal. "By all means," she said primly. "Let's push on."

He opened the door, and they went back out into the cold.

"A question," Tiffany said as she and Mitch left their third stop, a small farmhouse converted to a facility for developing cooking oils from various seeds. Why is everything so scattered? Wouldn't it make life easier if all the different branches of the company were under one roof, or at least concentrated in one area?"

"Definitely," Mitch said. "But for now, the situation is workable and affordable. The farm I grew up on wasn't as extensive as it is now. Pete and Jackie have been buying up neighboring properties, and rather than tear down the buildings, they've used them. There are more divisions downtown. Canfield Farm is a lot like Paradise Foods—diversified and spread out—but on a smaller scale." As they climbed onto the snow machine, he listed some of the company's holdings, giving Tiffany a thumbnail sketch of each.

When he started the motor, the talking had to stop. Tiffany was left to mull over what she'd learned. Unless Mitch was giving her an overly rosy picture of the way Canfield Farm had situated itself in the marketplace, it was just the kind of firm her company was eager to invest in.

The prospect of working for several months with Mitch's family during the merger was daunting. She wouldn't be able to avoid him—or *want* to. And he spelled trouble in a big way.

She decided to put those worries on hold for the moment. Nothing had been decided yet. Nothing would be decided for weeks. Instead, she concentrated on the ride itself, suddenly realizing that she was enjoying it. When had her nervousness evaporated?

The landscape fascinated her, its monochromatic starkness broken only by the brilliant azure of the sky and the metallic white-gold disk of the sun. It was like a different planet, alien but breathtakingly beautiful.

Tiffany knew she was storing up vivid memories that would stay with her for a long time to come, and when Mitch pointed out a white-tailed deer bounding toward a clump of evergreens, she forgot herself enough to tighten her arms around him in an impulsive hug.

She wondered if it was her imagination that the snowmobile seemed to slow down for a moment.

The morning flashed by too quickly. They were heading back to the farmhouse, and Tiffany found herself wishing they were just starting out.

Suddenly, when they were about a third of the way across a huge field lying to the west of the house, a violent gust of wind lifted the snow on the ground and sent it swirling like an airborne whirlpool, with Mitch and Tiffany and their snowmobile caught in the vortex.

Tiffany felt Mitch's body tighten and saw his head jerk as if he'd muttered a stream of explosive curses. Then he gunned the engine for extra speed, racing for the house.

But the gust was only a taste of what followed. Within moments the vehicle was hurtling blindly through an enveloping shroud of snow.

Tiffany was alarmed. She couldn't believe that conditions could change so fast, with so little warning, and she had no idea how Mitch could deal with them. Barreling ahead seemed dangerous. There were fences and tree stumps just waiting to be crashed into. Besides, visibility was nonexistent, so losing direction was almost inevitable. Stopping, however, didn't strike her as a better alternative. The prospect of being buried under a snowdrift was singularly unappealing.

She had only one option: To trust that Mitch *did* know what to do. Ducking her head behind his broad back for shelter from the stinging assault of wind and snow, she reminded herself that he knew the country, had grown up in it, and would manage somehow.

"Hang on!" he shouted over the howling wind and the reverberating buzz of the snowmobile.

Tiffany didn't have to be told twice. Her self-consciousness was forgotten as her arms and thighs tightened around him like vises. The machine veered sharply to the right. She didn't know why, and she didn't care. Mitch knew what he was doing, she kept chanting, squeezing her eyes shut.

All at once the wind's shrieks were muted, and it seemed to have stopped grabbing at her, trying to tear her away from Mitch and dump her off the snowmobile. Tiffany opened one eye and saw a tall, straight evergreen with branches that looked like arms. Outstretched, welcoming arms. She raised her head. More trees. Trees all around. Spruce and balsam, cedar and pine, laden with great mounds of whipped-cream snow, their colors ranging from pale, silvery emerald to clear jade to rich, dark teal. Interspersed among them, leafless branches coated with ice clicked as musically as crystal-drop chimes as they rubbed against one another.

Mitch had brought them to a perfect shelter, and Tiffany was entranced. She felt as if she'd been allowed into a secret place straight out of a fairy tale filled with snow princesses and ice castles.

Mitch cut the motor and pointed toward a small, barely noticeable structure tucked into the lowest branches of what Tiffany assumed was a huge old oak, or perhaps a maple.

"It's not bad right here," Mitch said, "but we might as well wait out the squall more comfortably." He looked back at Tiffany over his shoulder. "Think you can manage the snowshoes?"

Tiffany nodded absently as she peered at the wooden hut he'd indicated. "A tree house? We're going to wait in a tree house?"

"Sorry. It's the best I can do. And I apologize for not anticipating that little windstorm. I usually don't get caught short that way." He paused, then added almost inaudibly, "My mind wasn't on the weather, I guess."

"But a tree house?" Tiffany said excitedly. "Really? You mean, we can go up there?"

Mitch shot her a quizzical smile. "You sound as if you want to."

"I do! I wouldn't miss this chance for the world! I've never been in a tree house. Is it yours? Did you build it?"

Mitch laughed as he stepped off the snowmobile into the deep snow. "You're supposed to be scared or mad or at least a little upset, not thrilled," he said, retrieving the two sets of snowshoes and strapping on one pair. "What kind of southern tenderfoot are you, anyway?"

"The kind who intends to win a certain bet," she retorted, then grinned. "And the kind who's always wanted to see the inside of a tree house."

"I should have met you years ago. I'd have taken you up into my tree house anytime," Mitch said with his patented roguish wink.

"I'll just bet you would have," she drawled. "Along with every other female you could lure up there."

Mitch merely laughed and helped her off the machine and onto her snowshoes. The thought crossed his mind that he wished he *had* met Tiffany years before, but he pushed it away. If she'd been around when he was, say, twenty-three—when he'd been an idealist and a romantic, still believing there was one special woman meant for him—Tiffany would have been all of fifteen.

The thought made him feel like a cradle-robber, even though an eight-year span wasn't exactly a May-December gap. It just seemed that way because he'd changed so much in those eight years.

Besides, he reminded himself, he liked his free and easy existence. He hadn't planned for things to work out exactly as they had, but he was reasonably content, and he certainly wasn't looking to make any more changes in his life or himself.

He scowled, astonished that his thoughts had wandered down that particular lane. "Okay, let's go," he said with uncharacteristic gruffness. "Take short steps, like this." He demonstrated, then headed toward the tree, keeping an eye on Tiffany and noting with inordinate pleasure that she was a quick study.

After a few yards, Tiffany giggled. "And I thought diving flippers were difficult to manage. Walking on overgrown tennis rackets is interesting, to say the least."

He gave her a careful smile, approving but reserved. "You're doing fine. In fact, I'd say you have a lot of natural ability. You'd probably be a good skier."

"Do you really think so?" she said, beaming at him. "I do like waterskiing, you know. Is there much—?"

"Concentrate, Tiffany, or you'll . . ."

She tromped down on one snowshoe with the other and started to fall forward.

"Or you'll do that," Mitch said as his hand shot out to grip her arm and steady her.

After righting herself with his help, Tiffany laughed good-naturedly, then gave her full attention to reaching the tree without falling on her face.

Once they got there, Mitch tramped down a firm patch near the tree before undoing their snowshoes and driving them into the snow, where they remained upright. "I'll go up first to make sure the place is safe," he said. "It was a pretty solid little structure when Pete and I built it a couple of decades ago, and we check it regularly to make sure it's still okay in case the kids start coming here without telling us. But it's best to be careful."

Effortlessly climbing up to the small, square shack,

he pushed open its door and checked around a bit, then climbed back down. "Seems okay. I'll give you a boost so you can reach that first branch. Can you manage from there?"

"No problem." Tiffany grinned, pretending to spit on the palms of her mitts. "You should see me retrieve coconuts. Being from Hawaii doesn't make me a total incompetent, you know."

Mitch smiled and grasped her by the waist, lifting her until she could reach the branch and get a foothold.

His physical power amazed Tiffany—and excited her. The thought of his strong hands moving gently over her body, touching and stroking and arousing her, rekindled the inner flames she'd managed to tamp down while she'd been busy being terrified.

She ducked in through the low, open doorway. Inside, standing up straight was impossible, but otherwise the shelter seemed more than adequate. And it was everything she'd ever imagined a tree house would be—rough-hewn and totally masculine. Like the males who built it.

When Mitch joined her, Tiffany was opening the shutters of a small window on the side wall to let in some light. "Amazing. Shuttered windows," she teased. "I'm surprised there's no hot tub and media room."

"Hey, big brother and I were creating a serious hideaway, not some crummy lean-to. We were a couple of cool dudes," Mitch said with a self-mocking grin that abruptly changed to a frown as he bumped his head on the ceiling. "Man, this place has grown small over the years."

Tiffany laughed. "It's a wonderful spot for a boy," she said, dropping to her knees in the middle of the tiny room. "But did you and Pete actually build it yourselves?"

"With a lot of guidance from Dad, yes." Mitch followed Tiffany's lead, getting down on his knees as well. The room was so tiny, they were almost touching. He looked around. "We did a pretty good job, huh?"

"I have a feeling you and your brother don't do anything unless you do it well. Anything you put your hand to . . ." Her voice trailed off as heat surged through her like a flash fire. The very mention of Mitch's hands was enough to set her off. She looked around desperately for a quick change of topic. "You were a Tiger fan," she said, her glance coming to rest on several faded baseball posters on the wall.

"Still am. We get Detroit television here," he answered, watching her with an intentness that gave her butterflies.

He knew, Tiffany thought. He always knew what she was thinking and feeling . . . and wanting. She searched for something else to say. Spotting a crudely carved wooden sign hanging on another wall, she laughed. "Girls allowed," she read. "It's so *you*, Mitch."

"I seem to recall putting that up outside the door one day to bug Pete. He nearly banished me from the place. But he agreed not to beat me up when he saw this." Mitch reached out and turned the sign over to show what he'd printed on the reverse: NO girls allowed, NO exceptions, NO WAY!

Tiffany smiled, picturing Mitch finding countless ways to keep his older brother off balance. Pete was the serious one, Mitch the mischiefmaker. For a moment, she wondered how much of his roguish image was real and how much was pure teasing, but she quickly told herself not to slip into the trap of wishful thinking.

Realizing that she was losing herself in the depths of Mitch's dark eyes, she blinked and hugged herself, shivering.

"Are you cold?" Mitch asked gently.

Tiffany shook her head. "I don't think so. I'm not sure. Maybe a bit. I'm dressed warmly enough, but I guess my body hasn't adjusted to the climate yet."

"It hasn't had much chance. I should have had you put on more layers," he said, frowning. With a nod, he indicated the end wall. "C'mon," he said, moving to sit on the floor with his back against the wall. "Body heat's the best kind anyway." He tugged on Tiffany's hand to draw her close, then wrapped both arms around her.

As she rested her head on his shoulder, she silently agreed with him. Body heat was definitely the best kind. Mitch's body heat, in particular. "How long will it take for that wind to wear itself out?" she asked.

"Hard to say," Mitch answered. "Nervous?"

Tiffany hesitated. She rather liked being alone with Mitch in this hideaway. What she really wanted to know was how much time she could count on. But it wouldn't do to say so. "No, I'm not nervous," she told him. "Should I be? What happens if the storm gets worse?"

"There's an emergency kit in the snowmobile with a ground sheet, a hatchet, and a small propane heater. If it looks as if we're going to be here awhile, I'll make us a soft cocoon of balsam boughs and warm this shack up so much, you'll want to go outside to cool off."

Tiffany believed him. She was close to that point already. "And if we get hungry?"

"I think there are some candy bars in the kit."

"Candy bars?" Tiffany repeated, tipping back her head to glower up at him in feigned disapproval. "Candy bars in the emergency supplies of makers of health foods? I'm shocked. This might have to go into my report, Mr. Canfield."

"I assure you, they're wholesome candy bars," Mitch said, chuckling. "Made with dried fruit and nuts and sunflower seeds, or something. Jackie wouldn't allow junk food."

Tiffany laughed and hoped the storm would last awhile. She closed her eyes and imagined lying beside Mitch for hours in a forest-scented bed, with no sound but the wind singing through the branches, no light but whatever moonbeam could penetrate the dense grove, no reality crowding in on the blissful fantasy. She sighed and nestled closer to him.

They talked quietly for the next half hour or so, mostly about the farm and the old-fashioned upbringing Mitch and Pete had enjoyed there. She relished his tales of boyhood pranks and noticed that his humor was invariably at his own expense. In Mitch's stories, he played the clown while Pete came out as the hero— which made Mitch the hero in Tiffany's eyes.

"This place is lovely," she murmured as she sensed that the storm was dying down and her special moments with Mitch would be over soon. "You know what really gets to me around the farm?"

"What really gets to you?" Mitch asked softly.

"The silence," she whispered, as if reluctant to shatter the stillness. "It's almost a palpable thing, all velvety soft like a cushion against the rough edges of the world."

Mitch kissed the top of her head. "Do you know what gets to me around here?"

Tiffany looked up at him and shook her head.

His smile was heart-tuggingly tender. "You." Touching his lips to each of her eyelids, he went on, "You get to me, Tiffany Greer, whether you mean to or not, whether I want you to or not."

"Mitch," she whispered. "Oh, Mitch." She couldn't think of another thing to say, and in the next instant it didn't matter. His spice-scented mouth was covering hers, and somehow their gloves were gone and their caps were tossed aside, and she was lying over his lap, her arms around his neck and her fingers furrowing through the tousled silk of his hair.

"Tiffany," he murmured. "What am I going to do with you? I spend half my time making serious promises to myself that I'll keep my hands off you, and the other half breaking those promises."

"Break them," she urged. Her lips toyed with his. Her tongue coaxed his lips apart and delved eagerly into the delicious nectar of him. "Break those promises, Mitch. Just for a little while. No strings."

He surrendered to her soft entreaties and took her mouth in a deep, demanding kiss, but he suspected she was wrong. There were strings. There'd been strings since he'd first set eyes on her. Invisible but powerful threads drawing them together and binding them in an imprisoning web he was less and less certain he wanted to resist. The taste of her was intoxicating. Her unbridled desire was a potent aphrodisiac. With all the layers of nylon and padding and wool between them, the feel of her body pressing eagerly against his was the most erotic sensation he'd ever experienced.

When she began tugging at his clothes as if trying to get inside them, Mitch laughed hoarsely and undid both their jackets. Sliding his hand under her sweater and undershirt, he kneaded her breasts and teased their tips, exulting in the way they responded to his touch.

Tiffany arched her back, wanting more and more of his caresses. Her nipples were swollen, silently begging for his lips and tongue. Her whole body was alive as never before, tingling with need. Yearning to touch him, she pushed her hands under his clothes and stroked his back, his shoulders, his chest. She felt the stiffening of his taut nipples, the tightening of his muscles wherever she caressed him, the fiery warmth emanating from somewhere deep inside him.

The outside world ceased to exist. There was only Mitch. His touch, the warmth of his breath on her skin, his sweet, possessive kisses. She could have been in a South Sea island lagoon, for all that she noticed the cold. When Mitch's palm glided from the base of her throat all the way down to her waist, it left a burning path. When his fingers deftly unsnapped the waistband fastening of her ski pants and slid farther down, feathering over her belly and inching lower and lower, she thought her whole being was going to go up in flames. And when he found the sensitive epicenter of her desire and began caressing her with knowing fingers, she exploded like Mauna Loa, crying out his name over and over, the sound incoherent and muffled, lost in the recesses of his mouth.

"Lord, Tiffany," he said in a raspy voice. "Sweetheart, you're so ready for me, so . . ." His voice broke on a low, guttural groan. Tiffany's hand had made a bold push downward, and her fingers were curling around him as her hips rose to welcome his intimate invasion, opening to him as her mouth took the deep, rhythmic thrusts of his tongue.

But suddenly, a cold blast of frigid air battered the rough-hewn walls of the shack, sending swirls of snow through the cracks and the partly open window. Mitch released Tiffany's mouth and moved so that her hand slipped away from him. "No more," he said. "I'm right at the edge. I can't let this go on. I'm on the verge of stripping off all our clothes and taking you right here on the floor in the middle of a winter storm, and that's insane. Hell, it's downright dangerous! Let me hold you, sweetheart. I just want to hold you."

Tiffany was too far gone to do anything but obey. A tingling sensation was radiating out from her center in all directions, sizzling all the way to her toes, her fingers, the tips of her breasts, even her lips and the outer rims of her ears. Her arms and legs felt as if they were made of melted honey. Her skin was on fire, and the blood pounded in her temples so hard, there was a hollow roaring in her ears. And there was an ache inside her that felt as if it would never go away.

Mitch folded his arms around her. "It's all right, baby," he whispered. "It's okay." He kissed her forehead and temples and stroked her hair as if she needed comforting.

In an odd way, she did need comforting. She was deeply shaken. She'd never felt anything so intense and overwhelming before. She'd never dreamed she could be so abandoned. And all at once she was horribly shy. "I . . . I can't believe what just happened," she said raggedly.

"Neither can I," Mitch murmured. "I didn't mean it to happen. I seem to be saying that a lot since I met you, but it's true. My body has started to have a will of its own." He crooked his finger under her chin and lifted it, making an effort to smile down at her. "Anybody wanna strip down to their skivvies and go make angels in the snow?" he asked with a husky voice.

Grateful for his effort to defuse the tension, Tiffany managed a laugh. "I never thought I'd be tempted by an offer like that, but it sounds like a very good idea."

They were quiet for a few more minutes. Then Mitch, after listening intently to the receding wind, sighed heavily. "The storm seems to have settled down. We'd better go, Tiffany. If we don't, we might be crazy enough to stay, and our frozen bodies will be found tomorrow morning, locked together forever with blissful smiles on our faces."

Tiffany wrinkled her nose in mock distaste. "Your imagery is very persuasive, Mr. Canfield." She struggled to her feet and stood up on legs that felt boneless. "All set," she said brightly.

Fantasy time, she told herself, was over.

EIGHT

While Tiffany headed upstairs to change back to her jogging outfit, Mitch went into the kitchen, wondering why Jackie hadn't met them at the door and Rebecca was so quiet.

A slow cooker filled with steaming, homemade soup was waiting on the kitchen counter, along with a note from Jackie explaining that she'd taken Rebecca into town for some shopping and wouldn't be back until right before the sitter was due at one o'clock.

"Thanks a lot," he muttered. He hadn't expected to be left alone with Tiffany again once they reached the house. It was an extra complication and temptation in a morning filled with both.

"Are you hungry?" he asked when Tiffany returned to the kitchen.

"Starved," she said a little too cheerfully, striding over to stand beside him and peer into the soup pot, inhaling deeply. "I can't remember when I've ever been so famished."

"That's what you get for eating a sissy breakfast," Mitch said, reverting to teasing as his only remaining defense. Her cheeks were bright pink, her eyes sparkling, her hair charmingly awry. He wanted her so much, it hurt. "How about getting out some bread for us while I fill up a couple of bowls," he suggested.

Tiffany found a multigrain loaf in the bread box and began slicing it thinly. "I'll try porridge for breakfast tomorrow morning," she announced. "I've decided to start following your advice without arguing at every turn."

"I'll believe that when I see it," Mitch commented. He took two large soup dishes from the cupboard and put them on the counter, then frowned at what Tiffany was doing. "Hey, we need thick chunks of bread," he scolded.

Tiffany rolled her eyes. "Do you have to issue orders about everything? Some of us have to watch our diets, you know." She started to cut off another quarter-inch slice.

"So much for not arguing with me at every turn. That resolution lasted about as long as I expected it to." For which he was extremely grateful, Mitch added silently. Dumb arguments helped obscure what was really going on.

Tiffany moved the knife over another half inch. "Satisfied?" she asked after she'd cut a generous slice.

"It'll do," Mitch conceded, then couldn't think of

another thing to tease or argue or even chat idly about. His mind kept going back to the tree house, and judging by the way Tiffany's hand trembled from time to time and her tongue kept darting out to moisten her lips, she was having the same problem.

They sat across from each other at the kitchen table. All at once Tiffany came alive and started peppering Mitch with questions. Business questions. Farming questions. Marketing questions. It was as if she intended to bury the knowledge of shared intimacies under an avalanche of no-nonsense details.

He answered at length, going along with her pretense that there were no sensual undercurrents between them.

He was finishing the last spoonful of his second helping of soup, when he realized that she was unusually quiet. Probably bored by his tedious speech, he thought. Why not? *He* was.

He looked over at her, his brows raised questioningly. Her head had drooped forward, her eyes were closed. She was listing dangerously to one side.

Mitch was out of his chair and around the table in an instant. As if dimly aware that he was there, Tiffany let go completely and crumpled over onto his chest as he knelt down to catch her.

"What the devil am I going to do with you?" he murmured as he swept her up in his arms and carried her to the stairs. "I can't guarantee how often I'll put you to bed without joining you there, sweetheart. I'm only a man, and at the moment, not feeling especially honorable."

Tiffany's only response was to twine her arms around his neck and nuzzle her face into his throat.

He knew then that it was time for an a-man's-gotta-do-what-a-man's-gotta-do decision. And what he had to do was simple: Get out of town. He had business reasons to go anyway, but it was vital for him to do some hard thinking about this turn of events.

It wouldn't hurt Tiffany to have a breather as well, he told himself. She needed a chance to figure out whether she really felt something for him or was suffering confused and heightened emotions because she was exhausted.

He lowered her onto the bed, took off her shoes, pulled the comforter over her, and started to straighten up. But he stopped and bent down again, smoothing her hair back from her face and placing one light kiss on her forehead.

It wasn't easy to stand up again and force himself to go.

Never mind, he told himself firmly. A week or so on the slopes should clear his head. And by then, Tiffany probably would have decided once and for all that he was every inch the rogue she'd judged him to be from the start.

After three days of going over marketing figures with Jackie and operational details with Pete, Tiffany

DON'T HOLD BACK!

1. **No obligation!** No purchase necessary! Enter our Sweepstakes for a chance to win!
2. **FREE!** Get your first shipment of 6 Loveswept books, *and* a lighted makeup case as a free gift.
3. **Save money!** Become a member and about once a month you get 6 books for the price of 4! Return any shipment you don't want.
4. **Be the first!** You'll always receive your Loveswept books before they are available in stores. You'll be the first to thrill to these exciting new stories.

WINNERS CLASSIC SWEEPSTAKES
Entry Form

YES! I want to see where passion will lead me!

Place FREE ENTRY Sticker Here

Place FREE BOOKS Sticker Here

Enter me in the sweepstakes! I have placed my **FREE ENTRY** sticker on the heart.

Send me six *free* Loveswept novels *and* my *free* lighted makeup case! I have placed my **FREE BOOKS** sticker on the heart.

Mend a broken heart. Use both stickers to get the most from this special offer!

61234

NAME_____

ADDRESS_____ APT._____

CITY_____

STATE_____ ZIP_____

Loveswept's Heartfelt Promise to You!

There's no purchase necessary to enter the sweepstakes. There is no obligation to buy when you send for your 6 free books and free lighted makeup case. You may preview each new shipment for 15 days risk-free. If you decide against it, simply return the shipment within 15 days and owe nothing. If you keep the books, pay only $2.25 per book – a savings of $1.25 per book (plus postage & handling, and sales tax in NY and Canada). Prices subject to change. Orders subject to approval. See complete sweepstakes rules at the back of this book.

CD12

Give in to love and see where passion leads you!
Enter the Winners Classic Sweepstakes and
send for your FREE lighted makeup case and
6 FREE Loveswept books today!

(See details inside.)

Detach here and mail today.

was more enthusiastic than ever about the potential of Canfield Farm.

She'd arranged to move to a downtown hotel to be closer to the subsidiaries in the city.

"Are you sure you won't change your mind and stay here?" Jackie urged over a cup of coffee. They were waiting in the farmhouse kitchen for Pete to get back from the flour mill and drive Tiffany to her hotel. "We enjoy having you," Jackie went on. "And it really wouldn't be any trouble for one of us to drive you to town every morning and pick you up when you're through for the day."

Tiffany smiled, but shook her head. "I've loved being here, but I have a lot to do in the city. Part of my assignment is to estimate living costs, find out what's available in apartments, do a rundown on the life-style and amenities—all the nitty-gritty involved in settling someone here for a while if the deal goes through."

"Will that someone be you?"

"Perhaps." Tiffany took a sip of her coffee, then grinned. "In case you're wondering, I'm not going to let a daunting climate scare me off if I'm given a choice about staying." Or a daunting male who plays steamy games in frigid tree houses and then leaves without a word, she thought. "Unless my bosses have different plans for me, I'll be quite happy to stick with this project."

"Bravo," Jackie said, putting down her cup and applauding.

Tiffany realized that she'd become determined

about winning that bet with Mitch. She didn't care whether she showed *him* that she could cope with life in the north, but she wanted to show herself she could do it.

"Mitch will be pleased," Jackie said.

The remark startled Tiffany. Was another Canfield capable of reading her mind? "Where is he, anyway?" she asked, then wondered if it was possible to rip out her tongue retroactively.

"He's out on the West Coast helping the new manager of one of his ski resort shops get organized," Jackie explained. "Didn't he tell you he was going?"

Tiffany's eyes widened. "*One* of his shops?"

"That's right." Jackie hesitated, then smiled and shook her head. "I gather Mitch has been his usual never-explain self with you, Tiffany. Did he neglect to mention that he owns a whole chain of sporting goods outlets, as well as shares in a couple of very new, very popular ski resorts?"

Tiffany's insides began churning. "Mitch would have neglected to mention that he owns the store here in Winnipeg if I hadn't needed warm clothes," she said, drumming her fingertips on the table. She didn't care whether he owned every sporting goods store and half the ski resorts on the whole damn planet! What bothered her was that he'd been so determined to convince her he was devoid of ambition. Obviously he thought every woman who happened to be mildly attracted to him was a husband-hunting gold digger who'd be put off by his ski-bum routine.

"What bothers you more?" Jackie asked with a knowing smile. "The fact that Mitch is more successful than he lets on, or that he left town for a few days without telling you?"

"Neither," Tiffany answered, her chin thrusting up and out. "I think your brother-in-law is very . . . personable. But what he does, where he goes, and what he chooses to tell or not to tell couldn't matter less."

Jackie raised one brow. "No?"

"No," Tiffany said firmly.

"Too bad," Jackie murmured, then picked up her coffee cup and drained it.

Tiffany opened her mouth to ask Jackie what she meant by that cryptic comment, then clamped it shut. Some questions were better left unanswered.

Mitch felt a bit like a Shetland sheepdog trying to keep his flock together as he coaxed his budding cross-country skiers along the snow-covered center of the frozen Red River. They were headed toward The Forks, the spot where the Red met the Assiniboine in the heart of Winnipeg. The junction had evolved into a favorite recreation and shopping mecca for the denizens of the downtown area, as well as a tourist draw.

There were six people in Mitch's group, and he'd realized very quickly that all of them were fiercely determined to beat the odds that had been stacked against them by some trick of fate. He knew how they felt, but it was as important for him to teach them to be cautious as to spur them on. Pushing too hard could cause serious damage.

On this particular afternoon he was glad of the challenges presented by his new class. They kept his mind off Tiffany.

He smiled to himself. She'd just popped into his head again. She was doing that sort of thing all the time, never giving him a moment of peace, day or night. Leaving town hadn't helped, though he'd stayed away for more than a week. Hitting some of the toughest slopes in the West Coast mountains hadn't done any good, either. Working hard, playing harder, and indulging in a lot of girl-watching had been useless. No matter how many pretty women he'd forced himself to notice during the past nine days, he hadn't been able to see past the vivid memory of almond-shaped green eyes, a wonderful tangle of black hair, and a mouth so sweet, he seemed to have developed an incurable craving for it.

Time and again, he'd caught himself mentally replaying every conversation he'd had with Tiffany, laughing at her sassy rejoinders to his compulsive teasing, reacting painfully to the memory of the softness of her body and the addictive nectar of her kisses.

As he dropped back to the rear of the group to check on a straggler, he noticed a solitary skier about fifty feet back, trucking along with a great deal more determination than expertise. His heart turned over, for no better reason than that loner reminded him of Tiffany.

Things were really getting out of hand, he mused as

he gave his head a shake and returned his attention to his group. He saw that they could use a rest. "Okay, gang," he called. "Take five. Let's not get too frisky this first time out."

Grateful moans and groans greeted his call for a break.

Mitch grinned. "Hey, if you're that exhausted you should have let me know. A little whining doesn't hurt. Remember, we don't go for that no-pain-no-gain stuff around here. Nice and easy is our motto, okay?"

As his students laughed and began talking among themselves about how they were doing, Mitch couldn't resist stealing another peek at the slender figure coming up on the rear, head down in fierce concentration. She did remind him of Tiffany, even to the hot pink and black outfit she was wearing. It wasn't an uncommon style and color, he reminded himself as his pulse started skipping every second beat. And the odds of seeing his favorite Hawaiian puffing her way along the river were practically nil.

But as she came closer, he frowned. Was it possible that Tiffany would be cross-country skiing all by herself, late in the afternoon of a sixteen-below day?

No. Couldn't be.

Seconds later, Mitch's heart started performing a series of somersaults and back flips. The woman *was* Tiffany!

He skied over to her, executed a quick turn, and glided alongside her. "You want to win that bet this badly?" he said, priding himself on sounding reasonably offhand.

She looked up with a start, her eyes huge. "Mitch! What are you doing here?"

"Watch it," he warned. "You're going to trip yourself."

But it was too late. One of her skis skittered across the other, and one pole got tangled up between her legs while she drove the other into the snow behind her. She began swaying wildly, as if trying to decide between the two evils of pitching forward or falling back.

Mitch quickly transferred one of his own ski poles to the opposite hand, leaving himself a free arm to wrap around Tiffany's waist to steady her. It felt good to touch her again. So damn good, he didn't want to let her go. Ever. "You're okay now," he said, chuckling. "I've got you, sweetheart. I won't let you fall."

"I'll *never* get the hang of this!" Tiffany exploded. She leaned against Mitch for only a moment, then started battling to uncross her skis and sort out the poles. "Why in heaven's name would anyone go to all this effort and call it fun? It's not the least bit like waterskiing! It's hard work! And if you start in on me about not wearing that ski mask . . ."

"I won't. You don't need one today. There's not that much wind. And I should point out that one of the joys of cross-country skiing is that it *is* hard work. But it can be enjoyable if you have decent equipment and some idea of what you're doing." Mitch reached past Tiffany to extract the pole that was stuck in the snow behind her. Taking note of her flushed skin and the gasping for breath she was trying not to let him see, he asked, "Why didn't you tell me you wanted to learn?"

He realized his mistake as Tiffany looked up at him, a flash of anger in her eyes. He held on to the pole instead of giving it to her, in case she decided to take off—or break it over his head.

"I'd have had a little trouble finding you, wouldn't I?" she said in a deceptively reasonable tone. "You could give Casper The Friendly Ghost a run for his money with that disappearing act of yours. I didn't even know you were in town."

"I got back last night. Late last night," he said, frowning slightly as he wondered why he was explaining himself. He never explained himself. Not to anyone. And he suddenly realized something that was a bigger surprise. He was pleased—no, he was *thrilled*—that Tiffany was annoyed at him for going away. The situation was even more serious than he'd realized. "Where's Pete?" he demanded. "What's the matter with him, letting you come out here to teach yourself to ski?"

"I didn't tell him I planned to do this," Tiffany said. "I didn't see what there was to learn. You attach your feet to a pair of skis and start walking funny."

"What kind of wax did you use?"

Tiffany's forehead creased in a puzzled scow. "Wax?"

"That's what I thought. Sweetheart, cross-country skiing doesn't have to be this tough. You start with decent equipment that doesn't require a lot of fussing and is sized for you, not used rejects designed for a six-footer."

"Well, I wasn't about to spring for new gear when I had no idea how much use I'd get out of it," she said, glowering at him. "I saw an ad in the paper. The price was right, so I bought these things to get started."

Mitch grinned. He'd managed to get a rise out of Tiffany within minutes of seeing her again. For some reason, he loved riling her. Maybe it was because her eyes turned such a brilliant shade of green. Or because he'd missed that feisty little chin of hers. "How long have you been practicing?"

"An hour every afternoon for the past four days," Tiffany answered. "And I've survived. Amazing, isn't it?"

Mitch ignored her disgruntled irony. "How long have you been out today so far?"

"About forty minutes. Why?"

"I think you've subjected yourself to enough unnecessary punishment. My group's ready to call it a day, so we're about to head back. I assume you started out at The Forks."

"Your group?" Tiffany said, looking past him to the resting skiers she hadn't noticed until that moment. "You teach people how to do this? There's some trick to it? Besides having state-of-the-art equipment, I mean."

"I give them a few pointers," Mitch said. "Come with us. Maybe you'll pick up something useful."

She chewed on her lower lip, then shook her head. "I don't think I should. I'll slow you down."

"Don't be silly. You won't slow anyone down."

"Of course I will. Your people have had lessons. I haven't. They probably waxed their skis properly."

"As a matter of fact, they didn't need to. They're using fiberglass skis that don't require it. But apart from having decent equipment, my students have learned a far more important lesson."

"What's that?" Tiffany asked, curious.

"When *not* to be infernally independent. Let me put it this way, Tiffany: If you want to finish the run with two ski poles, you'll have to come with me."

She glared at him, trying to look annoyed but not managing very well. Her lips were curving in a tiny smile. "You have no scruples," she grumbled.

His grin was unapologetic. "You're catching on."

"When I first met you, you held my suitcases hostage so I wouldn't jump back on the plane while you were out getting your car," she reminded him. "Now it's a ski pole. What's next, my new skates?"

Mitch tipped back his head and laughed. "Say it isn't so. You haven't taken up skating too!"

"Not yet, but I'm going to. After all, little kids do it. How hard can it be?"

Groaning dramatically, Mitch said, "You're going to give me a lot of trouble, you know that?"

"I don't know any such thing. I'm not asking for your help. I don't even want your help."

"Well, you've got it whether you want it or not," he

informed her. "Starting right now. Are you coming, or do I have to resort to serious coercion?"

Tiffany thought about it, then nodded. "Oh, all right. If you're so hell-bent on being saddled with me, I'll join your class. But if one person laughs at me . . ."

"Nobody will laugh at you." Mitch handed her the hostage ski pole. "Believe me, there's not a soul in this group who would ever dream of laughing at anyone. All things considered, by the way, you were doing pretty well."

Tiffany brightened. "I was?"

"You were. And I admire you for going at it with such dedication."

She beamed at him. "Honestly?"

"Honestly," Mitch said, feigning exasperation but barely resisting the urge to haul her into his arms. "Now, scoot on ahead of me so I can check your form."

She darted him a quick, suspicious glance, but for once did as she was told without arguing.

Mitch followed right behind her, a crazy kind of happiness welling up inside him.

Tiffany's form, he mused as he watched her push her way toward the others, was fine. Very, very fine.

Tiffany had no doubt that Mitch was well aware of how shocked she'd been when she'd looked up from the ski trail and straight into his dark eyes, but she wondered if he had any inkling of the deep thrill she'd experienced, the inexplicable sense that all was right with the world again because he was there.

Yet if she'd dreamed for a moment that Mitch taught ski classes, she'd have stayed away from The Forks, a logical place for lessons. She was glad she hadn't known. Heaven help her, she was overjoyed to see him again even though she was still angry with him.

It occurred to her that this meeting might not be as accidental as it seemed. Jackie was the one who'd mentioned that the best time and place to practice skiing or skating was in the late afternoon at The Forks.

Interesting, Tiffany mused. Was Jackie trying to promote a romance? It seemed so. But why? Did she want her free-flying brother-in-law's wings clipped? And did she seriously believe that a Hawaiian canary could do it when countless northern chickadees must have tried and failed?

Impatient with herself for allowing such foolish ideas to stray into her mind, Tiffany swept them aside and concentrated on keeping her skis untangled.

To her surprise, she kept up with Mitch's group without much difficulty, and didn't feel like an interloper. She was welcomed by smiles and words of encouragement from everyone, and even a few flattering comments about how advanced she was compared to the rest of them.

By the time the run was over and she was removing her skis, Tiffany understood why Mitch had been able to promise that nobody would laugh at her. Each one of his students had a great deal more to overcome than inexperience.

As she stood up to strap her skis and poles together, Tiffany surreptitiously watched Mitch moving from one person to the next, offering congratulations for special accomplishments and making suggestions for practicing between classes.

She heard spontaneous expressions of appreciation being heaped upon him, and she saw how he tried to brush off all the thanks with a wisecrack.

She felt her heart expanding until she thought it was going to burst. More than once her eyes grew moist because Mitch, in his own irreverent way, was so caring, kind, and compassionate.

But she wanted more than ever to throttle the man.

"You're not a flake, Mitch Canfield," she said when everyone else had left. She picked up her skis, lifted them to one shoulder, and marched over to him on wobbly legs. "You're a fake. A fake flake, that's you."

He grinned and caught her thrust-out chin in his gloved hand. "Why? Because I teach skiing? It's a great way to build business for the store, don't you think? I'm creating my own customers. And I get to pretend I'm working when I'm really out having a good time."

"You're not building business," she said, pulling her chin free of his gentle grasp. "You're building bodies. Damaged bodies. Your classes are therapy sessions. I suppose you're an M.D. as well as an M.B.A."

"Hardly. I'm just helping a physiotherapist friend

with his patients. He was there for me, far beyond the call of duty, when I needed him a few years back. I'm trying to pass along the favor."

Tiffany cocked her head to one side and frowned. "Helped you? How? When? Did you have some debilitating illness? Were you hurt in some kind of accident?"

Mitch's careless grin took on the devilish sparkle that always made Tiffany's knees go weak. "Hold on, sweetheart. If you want answers to those questions, you'll have to have dinner with me."

"Fine," Tiffany said without hesitation. "Where and what time?"

Mitch was visibly taken aback. "You mean, I don't have to bully you into it?" Bending his knees until his face was on a level with hers, he peered into her eyes. "You're not mad at me anymore?"

"Mad at you?" Tiffany said, playing innocent. "Not at all. But make no mistake about it, I accepted only because I'm curious about you. You're an interesting enigma. But I've become immune to your fatal charms. Totally immune, understand?"

"Oh good," he said, pretending to mop his brow in relief as he straightened up. "Then I assume you wouldn't feel threatened if I suggested dinner at my place? Just the two of us, a bottle of good wine, a blazing fire, soft music in the background? After all, given this immunity of yours, what could happen?"

"I'd feel very threatened, and you know perfectly

well what could happen," Tiffany said, refusing to be tempted.

"Okay, then, we'll go out somewhere. I'll drive you back to your hotel, leave you there to change, then pick you up and take you to some great little place nearby."

Tiffany frowned. "How did you know I'd moved to a hotel?"

For once, Mitch was nonplussed. "Well, I . . . I happened to drive out to the farm this morning. I wanted to deliver some presents I'd picked up for the kids." With sudden haste, he removed Tiffany's skis from her shoulder and hefted them onto his own, along with his gear. Cupping his free hand under her elbow, he started propelling her along beside him toward the riverbank. "No sense standing around talking when we could be on our way," he muttered.

Tiffany didn't balk. It occurred to her that Mitch's gruff bossiness usually appeared in a situation that made him uncomfortable. She couldn't help wondering about his morning visit to the farm. Had he expected to see her there? Perhaps even hoped to see her? Had he been disappointed to find that she'd gone?

Oh, right, she told herself. *Get real*. "Do you mind telling me where we're headed?" she asked.

"To my car. It's in the parking lot across the way. Which reminds me. How did you get here with those skis? Cabs normally don't have racks for carrying them."

"I walked."

"You walked?" He sounded indignant. "From where?"

"From the hotel. It's only about ten minutes from here."

"Carrying your skis?"

"You told me not to rent a car until I'd acquired a few winter-driving skills," she reminded him. "And I haven't had time for lessons. Besides, the walk to the river was a good warm-up exercise."

"And the trek back to the hotel afterward?"

She grinned. "An excellent cool-down," she said, then relented. "Okay, I admit my legs were a little shaky."

"Just a little," Mitch muttered. "From now on, I'll take you skiing or skating or wherever you want to go."

"Why?" Tiffany asked. The man had committed all sorts of lies of omission so she wouldn't become too interested in him. He'd left town without bothering to tell her he was going. He wasn't offering a word of explanation now that he was back. Yet here he was, being his usual protective, autocratic self, behaving as if he were personally responsible for her. "Why should you put yourself out to help me win a bet—and help yourself lose it?" she persisted when he didn't answer.

"Because that stupid bet has made you think you have to prove how tough you are."

"I don't have to prove anything. I *know* how tough I am."

Mitch stopped dead, swung both sets of skis and poles down from his shoulder, and drove them into a snowbank. He turned to Tiffany and grasped her by the upper arms to pull her against him. "I know how tough you are too," he said softly. "Tough to forget." His mouth closed over hers as he folded his arms around her. His tongue parted her lips and probed behind them. It was a hot, deep, demanding kiss that dissolved every shred of resistance Tiffany tried to muster. She surrendered helplessly at first, then eagerly. She slid her arms around Mitch's waist, the slick fabrics of their jackets rustling with the friction of the movement. As warmth from his body surrounded her, she absorbed it, letting it sink in until patches of ice hidden far inside her began to thaw.

"Tiffany," Mitch murmured, gently touching his lips to the corners of her mouth. "Tiffany, do you have any idea what you do to me?"

"No," she answered. "Tell me."

"You confuse me. You drive me crazy. You haunt me," he said, raining kisses on her upturned face. "What's happening between us? *Why* is it happening?"

"I don't know." Tiffany kissed the underside of his jaw and tasted the fragrant spice of his skin with the tip of her tongue. "Opposites attract, maybe?"

He laughed huskily, reaching up with one hand to push her head down onto his chest and cradle it there. "Maybe. But whatever's going on, it's potent stuff. I tried denial. It didn't wash. I tried running away. All I accomplished was to realize that I missed you. Dammit, I *missed* you!"

Tiffany was about to admit the same, but as the

drugging effects of his kiss wore off a little she remembered that Mitch Canfield was very good at whatever he did, and what he was doing at the moment was seducing a woman whose claim of immunity had presented him with an irresistible challenge.

It wasn't a pleasant thought, but it seemed to Tiffany that it was a realistic one. She summoned all her willpower, twisted out of his arms, and marched over to the skis while he watched her, frowning. "You don't have to say things like that," she told him with a forced smile as she lifted her skis to her shoulder—though the smile was more for her own benefit than for his. She'd turned her back on him. "You've made your point. If you decide we're going to have an affair, I suppose we'll have an affair. But it would be better if we didn't, because we can't count on an easy, built-in ending to a harmless fling. I hope to stay around for a while, working with Jackie and Pete."

"I know that," Mitch said, sounding annoyed. "Jackie told me this morning. But I wasn't counting on an easy, built-in ending. How could I? I wasn't counting on a beginning!"

As she heard the squeak of dry snow, Tiffany knew Mitch was moving toward her. She whirled around, then gasped in horror as he had to duck to avoid being clipped by her skis.

He reached up and took them from her. "I'll carry your weapons, if you don't mind," he said tersely. "Decapitation doesn't appeal to me. How many headless bodies are lying around between here and the hotel?"

"A baker's dozen," she snapped. "All of them arrogant males who could stand to be cut down to size!"

He tossed her skis, along with his own, up to his shoulder. "Well, you're just the lady who can do it," he muttered.

Tiffany watched, fascinated, as angry flames appeared in his eyes, then flickered and changed. Suddenly the flames were dancing lights, alive with humor and something else she couldn't identify. "Yeah," he said, grinning and draping an arm around her shoulders. "You're definitely the lady for that job. Now, shall we take up where we left off before you distracted me? Let's go get changed so we can find someplace to eat."

Tiffany was stunned by the quick change in him. "You still want to go out with me for dinner?"

"Why not? I'm hungry. Aren't you?"

"I give up," she said, rolling her eyes.

"Give up what?"

"Trying to understand you. Trying to keep up with your quicksilver moods. Trying to figure out which Mitch is the real Mitch."

He laughed and hugged her a little closer. "Funny, I was just thinking about giving up on that one myself."

She waited for him to explain.

As usual, he didn't.

NINE

Something about Mitch was different, Tiffany thought after he'd dropped her off at the hotel to freshen up before dinner. It wasn't any specific change she could put her finger on. She sensed a subtle alteration in him that was both intriguing and unsettling.

After a quick shower, she put on the cream slacks and peach cowl-necked sweater she'd bought the day before. Surprisingly, she liked the feel of soft wools and knits against her skin, and she definitely approved of the way her new clothes kept their crisp, well-tailored look throughout the day. One distinct advantage of a cold climate over a torrid one was that she didn't have to battle the rumpled look caused by heat and humidity.

She put the finishing touches to her hair and makeup, sprayed on a light cloud of perfume, and checked her watch. Mitch was due any minute.

Her phone rang. She smiled as she picked up the receiver. Naturally he would be right on time. "Hi, Mitch," she greeted him.

There was a pause before he spoke. "Hi," he said. It was a low, husky sound, as intimate as a whisper. "I'm here. Should I come up, or will you come down?"

A shiver skimmed down Tiffany's spine, as if his lips had touched the nape of her neck and his breath had tickled her skin. "I'm ready," she said, a catch in her voice. "I'll be right there."

She hung up and quickly pulled on her new cream leather ankle boots, wondering if Mitch would approve of them. Then she grabbed her coat and handbag and hurried out to the elevator. She was halfway to the ground floor when she suddenly realized what was happening. She and Mitch were having a date. He wasn't doing his brother or Jackie a favor by playing chauffeur or tour guide. He was taking her out for dinner, just the two of them.

Excitement bubbled inside her like the fizz in champagne. Smiling as the elevator doors slid open, she vaguely noticed a tall man standing to one side of the doors, but she didn't look directly at him as she rushed toward the lobby, eager to be with Mitch.

Hearing a deep, familiar chuckle, she stopped, slowly turned, and stared in astonishment at the *Gentleman's Quarterly* type she'd brushed past. "Mitch!"

He laughed and reached out to take hold of her two hands, pulling her toward him. "Why the surprise?"

"You! I mean, my goodness, you're . . ." Lost for

words, she gazed at him, taking in the cashmere top-coat that was open over a rich tweed sport jacket, ivory crewneck sweater, and beautifully tailored slacks. "You're all dressed up," she said at last.

"I must have looked pretty grubby the other times you saw me if you think this is dressed up," he remarked, tucking her hand under his arm. "Do you have to act so shocked?"

"You've never looked grubby," she protested as he led her through the lobby. "You're . . ." She laughed and shook her head, then pretended to glower at him. "You're gorgeous whatever you're wearing, and you know it."

"Speaking of gorgeous," he said, giving her a quick once-over, "have you been shopping?"

"I have." She kicked out one foot in a goose step. "Pretty but practical boots. Lined. Only ankle-high, but they do have good treads on the soles." Reaching into her pocket, she found her new gloves and pulled them out to show him. "Also lined. I'm learning."

"Good. But you're still wearing the daffodil coat."

"I cope by layering under it, except for tonight, when I knew I'd be with a gentleman who spoils me rotten by making sure his Cherokee is cozy before he lets me get into it. Coats are expensive. I want to be sure I'll be staying here long enough to need a new one before I spend that kind of money."

"And when do you expect to be sure?" Mitch asked as they reached the lobby's exit doors.

"I've sent a preliminary report to Honolulu and I'm

waiting for a reaction." She gave Mitch an amused look as he started buttoning up her coat. "I could do that, you know."

Mitch frowned. "I guess you could." He finished the job anyway. "You aren't wearing a scarf," he scolded.

"I said I was learning, not that I'd graduated," she retorted. Yet she couldn't stop smiling, unexpectedly finding that she enjoyed the way Mitch fussed over her. His instinctive, almost absentminded protectiveness no longer struck her as condescending. It made her feel treasured.

Half an hour later she found herself nibbling calamari in a Mediterranean-style bistro. She'd anticipated an interrogation about the report she'd sent her company on Canfield Farm, but Mitch didn't appear to want to talk business. He seemed more interested in learning about her, coaxing her into revealing more about Tiffany Greer than she'd ever told anyone, more than she thought anyone would ever want to know. She didn't tell him, however, about the man who'd taught her to be careful where she placed her trust. At his best, Trevor Blake had been a little like Mitch, and the slight resemblance made her uncomfortable. For this one evening, she didn't want to wonder whether Mitch was like Trevor at his worst.

When she got around to asking Mitch about the physiotherapy he'd needed, he simply answered, "I had a skiing accident." With a grin and a wink, he added,

"It happens, even to the best of us. Speaking of skiing, I'll bet you're a real champ on water skis."

Okay, Tiffany thought, so he didn't want to talk about it. She wouldn't push. "Not a champ, but not as clumsy as I am on snow," she said with a laugh, and went on to talk about the inspiring people she'd met that day in his class.

It slowly dawned on her that she was being courted. It was an old-fashioned word, she mused, but an accurate one. Mitch was wooing her. He made her feel as if no other woman existed for him. His teasing was gentle, not laced with challenge. There were no mixed messages, no moments of barely leashed desire interrupted by a cavalier pulling back. He was witty, flattering, and even affectionate. If he was setting the scene for seduction, he was doing a good job.

When he saw her to her room, Tiffany wondered if he had some expert ploy up his sleeve to get himself invited inside. She found herself hoping he did.

His ploy *was* expert, and typically direct. When she opened her door, he simply walked into the room with her and closed the door behind them. But his comment as he looked around was less than romantic: "This won't do," he said, scowling. "This is no good at all."

Standing with him inside the door, Tiffany followed his gaze with a puzzled smile. "What won't do? What's no good?"

"This room. It's not even a suite."

"Junior execs don't rate suites," she pointed out.

"I'll have to wait until I'm the company president before I get that kind of luxury."

"And is being a company president your burning ambition?" Mitch asked, skewering her with his dark eyes.

"Isn't it everybody's?" she asked, fully aware that there were all sorts of people who didn't aspire to corporate stardom—including herself. But she realized that she rather liked getting Mitch's hackles up. The evening had been too pleasant. She missed the sparks. Besides, she still had a bone to pick with the man. "Even you have more ambition than you admit," she pointed out. Turning to give him her most innocent smile, she asked sweetly, "How many ski shops are there in your chain, anyway?"

He lifted one brow. "Does it matter?"

"Not in the least. In fact, I'd rather you didn't tell me. Your image as an irresponsible hedonist has been tarnished enough by that business degree of yours, not to mention by that trip you took out west to help your new manager get organized, and by your volunteer work as a lay therapist. If I knew any more good things about Mitch Canfield than I've already learned, I might get certain outlandish ideas he doesn't like his women to entertain."

His eyes narrowed as he started toward her. "You know, I like the sound of that," he said in a lazy drawl.

Tiffany's guard shot up. "That sound of what?"

"That 'his women' phrase. Especially when you put yourself in that category—"

"It's just an expression," Tiffany cut in hastily, backing away from him.

His grin was more insolent than ever. "Just an expression? Are you certain?"

"Of course." The backs of her calves hit the bed. She wondered if her subconscious had planned the whole maneuver. Wasn't she happier having her rogue back instead of the perfect gentleman Mitch had been all evening? Didn't she want him to throw caution to the wind and her onto the bed?

Whatever her subconscious had planned, however, her conscious mind flew into a panic. "I certainly didn't expect you to take what I said literally," she said, hearing a note of desperation in her voice. She tried going on the offensive. "You're using evasive tactics, Mitch Canfield. You're trying to obscure the fact that you . . . you *insulted* me."

He reached out and started undoing the buttons of her coat. "How did I insult you, sweetheart?"

"By making two arrogant, egotistical assumptions," she said, riveted by the adroit movements of his fingers, somehow unable to lift a hand to stop him. "First, you decided you were so irresistible that I—"

"Irresistible?" he interrupted as he finished with the buttons and slid his hands inside her coat to span her waist. "That reminds me. Have I mentioned how pretty and touchable you look tonight? That peach color is nice. You glow in it. We hardly needed a candle at our table." Dipping his head, he caught her earlobe between his teeth and nibbled gently while his thumbs lightly stroked the undersides of her breasts through her sweater. "But I interrupted," he murmured after a moment. "You were saying?"

Tiffany tipped back her head as he trailed hot, moist kisses along the side of her neck. "Saying?"

"About how I insulted you by making two arrogant, egotistical assumptions," he reminded her. His thumbs strayed toward the tips of her breasts, flicking back and forth, teasing them until the taut nubs were thrusting aggressively against the soft knit of her sweater. "My first assumption seemed to have something to do with thinking I was irresistible," he murmured. "So irresistible that you . . ." He paused to kiss his way along the underside of her jaw to a tender spot below her chin, then asked in a husky whisper, "So irresistible that you what, Tiffany?"

"I don't remember," she said, her patience fraying as she slid her arms around Mitch's waist and pushed her hands under his sweater. "I'm hot. Too hot to be able to think."

"I know," Mitch said, touching his mouth to hers. "Beautifully, excitingly hot."

"That's not what I mean," she protested raggedly. "It's my coat. I'm sweltering in it."

Mitch chuckled, and a moment later her coat was lying over the foot of the bed. "Better?" he asked, teasing her lips with nibbles and caresses.

She answered by curling her arms around his neck and slowly stroking her tongue back and forth over his bottom lip. Thrilled by his groan of desire, she felt a rush of feminine power. She wanted to drive him as crazy as he was driving her.

But all at once he was curving his hands around her shoulders and holding her away from him. "I think I'd better get out of here," he said, his voice thick and his breathing unsteady. "If I stay, I'll make love to you, and I don't want to do that. Not here, and not yet."

"Why?" Tiffany demanded, too frustrated to be more diplomatic.

"Good question," Mitch said with a smile. "We're finally alone without danger of being interrupted at an untimely moment. We don't have to worry about freezing to death. But I guess I'm more of a romantic than I thought. I don't want our first lovemaking to take place in a utilitarian little hotel room, and I'd like to know there's something between us besides strictly physical attraction."

She blinked. "And you call yourself a rogue?"

"No," he said, his eyes twinkling. "*You* called me a rogue."

Frowning, Tiffany tried to take a step back and twist out of his grasp. But the bed was still right behind her, and Mitch wasn't letting go. "Why did you kiss me the way you did if you're going to call a halt to things when I'm ready to make a fool of myself?"

"Look, I'm not a saint," he said, turning serious. "And you weren't even close to making a fool of yourself. You're beautiful and sensuous, and I didn't know what real wanting was until you came into my life. Tiffany, I'm not playing games. I'm going for the gold here. I learned a long time ago that when you do that, you have to be very sure you're ready, or you could kill your chances and get hurt in the bargain." He kissed the tip of her nose, took a deep breath as if gathering his strength, then moved away from her and headed for the door. With his hand on the knob, he turned and took one last, yearning look at her, then quietly closed the door behind him.

A pillow sailed across the room and hit the door with a dull thump ten seconds later.

Tiffany was at work bright and early the next morning after a long night of too little sleep and too much thinking.

Her temporary office in the company's midtown packaging plant was small and strictly functional, but it provided a desk, a phone, an assistant, and access to a fax and whatever other equipment she might need. Unfortunately, it didn't feature a button she could press to clear her mind of Mitch.

The phone rang at ten o'clock, jarring her from one of many unintentional reveries and reminding her that she'd lost her concentration—again.

"Okay, I've got a house for you," Mitch announced as soon as Tiffany had said hello.

She stared at the receiver. "What in heaven's name are you talking about? And how did you know where to get in touch with me?"

"Jackie told me," he said, answering her second

question first. "And I'm talking about your living accommodations. Say the word, and I'll drive you over to have a look at the place. You can move in today, if you like."

"Move in where?"

"To the house, of course."

Tiffany rolled her eyes. "Oh, of course. The house." She decided to try asking more specific questions. "Would you mind telling me what house we're talking about, why I should take a look at it, and why I can move into it today?"

After a heavy sigh, Mitch said, "It belongs to a friend of mine. A couple of weeks ago he asked me to keep an eye on it and water his plants while he basks in the Arizona sun for the rest of the winter. I called him this morning to ask how he'd feel about having a live-in sitter who'll keep his jungle healthy instead of a vegetation-killer dropping by every once in a while. He told me to hand over the keys, the sooner the better. Those plants seem to mean a lot to him."

"You threatened to murder his plants unless he allowed a total stranger to move into his house?"

"No, I told him that I'd discovered I don't have a green thumb, even with the best of intentions and the long list of instructions he gave me. Your *are* good with plants, aren't you?"

"Yes, but—"

"Terrific. I knew you would be. Now, to get back to the point, you should take a look at the place as soon as possible. It's crazy to spend another night in that cramped room when you can enjoy a nice home and do a favor for a snowbird and his sick plants at the same time. What time should I pick you up?"

As usual, Tiffany couldn't decide whether she'd rather hug Mitch or strangle him. She couldn't deny the thrill it gave her to hear his voice, let alone to know he was thinking about her and arranging for her to be more comfortable, but he was so maddening! How could he call and act as if there wasn't the slightest bit of tension between them? How could he sound so breezy after walking out on her the night before, knowing perfectly well that he was leaving her in a state of acute physical and emotional frustration?

"Tiffany, are you still there?"

"Yes," she answered with a start. "Sorry. I was distracted." She frowned, wondering why she was apologizing and making excuses. Enough, she decided. She was going to tell Mitch Canfield to quit trying to manage her life.

"That's okay," he said before she could utter a word. "Why don't I come by around eleven-thirty? I'll drive you over to see the house, and afterward we can go for lunch."

Tiffany opened her mouth, ready to erupt at him for being such a steamroller, but closed it again as a stack of files she'd requested arrived in the arms of Cindy Lawson, the secretary who'd been pulled from the company's typing pool to be her temporary assistant. "Thanks, Cindy," Tiffany murmured.

"Sweetheart, I've obviously called at a bad time,"

Mitch said. "I'll let you go. See you at eleven-thirty, okay?"

Tiffany was too slow. When she simply stared at the receiver, trying to decide how to put him in his place, he apparently took her silence as agreement and hung up.

At eleven-twenty, Tiffany was chewing nervously on her bottom lip, drumming her fingertips on her desk, and checking her watch every two minutes.

Trying to prepare a set of graphs as a follow-up to her initial report, she'd closed her door so she wouldn't be distracted by the phone calls she'd asked Cindy to make, but the work wasn't going well. She was squandering her concentration on Mitch. On what to say to him when he arrived. On whether to tell him to back off.

The very fact that he was undermining her professionalism was reason enough to set things straight between them. He popped into her mind at the most inconvenient moments, and it had been happening since the very beginning.

In the evenings, when she tried to relax in a bubble bath, he was there, soaping her body with slow, sensual strokes that left her shuddering with need. In the middle of the most mundane conversations, she would be listening attentively one minute, then absently touching her lips the next, recalling the dizzying sweetness of Mitch's kisses.

She was a bundle of erotic energy that had to be dispersed in some harmless fashion before it blew up and caused some real damage.

There was a light tap on her door. "Yes?" she said, unbidden excitement surging through her like a shot of amphetamine.

Cindy poked her head in. "Mr. Canfield's here," she said, looking nervous and wide-eyed.

Tiffany frowned. Cindy was a very pretty, very curvy blonde, about nineteen years old. The kind of nubile young thing who would be dazzled by Mitch, the kind he undoubtedly turned on his charm for, if only to stay in practice. For that matter, he probably didn't know how to turn it off. "Eleven twenty-two," she muttered. "He's early."

"I didn't know he was expected," Cindy said in a breathy Marilyn Monroe voice. She slipped into the office and pushed the door shut behind her. "I'm new with the company. I've never seen Mr. Canfield before. Golly, everything the other girls said is true. He's gorgeous!"

Tiffany got to her feet and went to stand at the window behind her desk, facing out. "Is he?" she said, trying to sound bored. "I hadn't noticed."

Cindy giggled. "Really? No kidding? Wow!"

Tiffany closed her eyes. Wow? Good lord. "Please ask Mr. Canfield to come in," she said, fixing her gaze on the traffic three stories below. Cindy's reaction to Mitch had stiffened her own resolve to resist his appeal.

She didn't turn when she heard her door open and

shut, or when she heard him greet her with a casual, "Hi there." If she looked at the man, she couldn't trust her knees not to buckle. Worse, she might rush into his arms, melt against him, and sigh a helpless, "Wow."

"Good morning," she said with deliberate formality, keeping her eyes on the busy street traffic. "Before you say anything, I want to tell you that I'm very appreciative of all your efforts on my behalf, but I do not appreciate your autocratic attitude. Furthermore, I wish you'd get it into your domineering male head that I'm not your responsibility. The suitability of my clothing is not your responsibility. My accommodations are not your responsibility. So please, let me do my job, make my own mistakes, and decide for myself the little details like where I'll stay while I'm here, all right?"

There was a silence of several seconds, then a stunned, "I don't get it. What did I do?"

Tiffany froze. That voice. There was the slightest difference. . . .

Whirling, she felt a blush sweep over her. "Pete!"

He cocked one brow. "Who'd you think it was? I heard Cindy tell you I was—" Stopping abruptly, he grinned. "Mitch?"

Tiffany groaned and went back to her chair. She sank onto it, burying her face in her hands. "Would it do any good to apologize?"

"No, because it isn't necessary." Pete sat down in the chair facing her. "I was in the plant checking on some new cereal packaging, so I thought I'd stop by to see whether you were getting all the cooperation you need."

Tiffany nodded, then lowered her hands, and faced Pete. "Before you ask, let me assure you that Mitch hasn't done anything untoward."

"Except upset you, apparently. What has he been—?"

Pete was interrupted as Cindy poked her head in again. "There's *another* Mr. Canfield out here!" The girl's eyes were china-blue saucers, sparkling with barely controlled excitement. "Should I show him in too?"

"By all means," Tiffany said, suppressing a giggle that was half amusement, half nervous tension.

Cindy showed Mitch in a few seconds later, dimpling up at him and batting her eyelashes. Tiffany was amazed. She hadn't realized that women actually did that sort of thing. She hoped *she* didn't, though she wasn't sure what she was capable of when Mitch was around.

Cindy left the room as reluctantly as a child being sent to bed just when an adult party was getting interesting. As soon as she'd closed the door behind her, Pete stood up and turned to Mitch. "I'm glad you're here, little brother. I was asking Tiffany what you'd done to upset her, but now you can tell me yourself."

Mitch looked at Tiffany. "Are you upset about something?"

"Only that I seem to have a bad habit of mistaking your brother for you," she answered.

"That's an extremely bad habit," Mitch said, his eyes dancing. "It could get you into a lot of trouble with Jackie. And with me, I might add."

Tiffany shot out of her chair and put her hands on her desk as she leaned over it. "I didn't mean it that way."

"What way?" Pete asked.

Mitch grinned at her. "Yes, Tiffany, what way?"

Straightening up, she hesitated, considering the feasibility of diving out the window. If there was no snowbank outside to break her fall, it didn't matter. She was going to die of embarrassment anyway. "I was asking you to consider the possibility that I'm capable of managing my own life. Unfortunately it turned out that I was talking to Pete."

"We don't look that much alike," Mitch commented, glancing at his older brother. "He's bigger. I'm cuter."

Pete snorted and rolled his eyes.

"I didn't see Pete," Tiffany explained through clenched teeth. "I was at the window when he came in, and I started talking without turning around."

Mitch chuckled with great satisfaction. "Couldn't look me in the eye when you were telling me to butt out, huh? Didn't I warn you a long time ago to watch where you're going? That advice applies as well to tearing a strip off somebody as to tearing out of an airport onto an icy sidewalk."

Tiffany glared at him, her mouth working to form a retort that wouldn't come. Finally she made a growling sound deep in her throat, sank back down onto her chair, and rested her chin on both fisted hands. "Pete, if you ever find your brother planted headfirst in a field of deep snow, you'll know who did it," she grumbled.

"Will somebody please tell me what's with you two?" Pete said, looking from one to the other. "You have a language all your own. Jackie seems to understand your conversations, but I can't follow them."

"Tiffany finds me a little bit bossy at times," Mitch explained.

"Attila The Hun was a little bit bossy," Tiffany shot back. "You're—"

"Trying to make your life easier," Mitch cut in. "Don't you get it? I want you to win the bet."

Tiffany stared at him, a soft warmth suddenly pervading her body. He wanted her to decide she could cope with Winnipeg. He wanted her to stay. "You do?" she murmured after a long, charged moment.

"What bet?" Pete asked, looking as if he was about to start throwing things. Or people.

Mitch turned to his brother. "I've arranged for her to use John Kozak's house instead of staying in a hotel," he offered as a partial explanation.

"No kidding? John Kozak's house?" Pete turned to Tiffany. "What are you waiting for? Grab it!"

Tiffany looked at the two men for a moment, then sighed. One Canfield was enough to deal with. Two of them added up to a lost cause. "You're right," she said, getting to her feet and striding over to the tiny closet where her coat was hanging. "What am I waiting for?"

Mitch had opened the closet by the time she reached it. As he pulled out the yellow coat and held it up to Tiffany, he let his gaze slide over her, somehow making his expression both critical and appreciative. "Nice suit," he commented. "Red's terrific on you. But it's not what I'd call layering under your coat. What about a warm sweater in place of that flowered silk blouse?"

Tiffany shoved her arms into her coatsleeves. "Since I take cabs all the time, this coat is fine, and I don't need to pile on a lot of extra clothes under it. Besides, it's only seventeen below outside today." She shot Pete an imploring look. "Do you see why I get a little testy with this man? My *mother* never nagged me the way he does. He—" Turning to face Mitch, she stopped talking abruptly. He was beaming at her, his smile so dazzling, it took her breath away.

"Only seventeen below," Mitch said softly. "*Only.* You didn't even know what you were saying. Honey, when you decide to win a bet, you go all the way."

Tiffany stared at him, her eyes widening. "Good grief, am I turning into a *northerner*?"

Mitch laughed and reached out to cup the back of her neck with one hand. "I'll go get the Jeep and drive it up to the door while you put on your boots," he murmured, then brushed his lips over hers in a kiss that was as boldly possessive as it was gentle. Raising his head, he gave her another smile that melted every bone in her body, and released her. "See you later, Pete," he said casually as he sauntered to the door.

"Right. Sure. Later," Pete mumbled.

Shaking herself from a daze after Mitch had gone, Tiffany looked at Pete with a smile and a what's-a-person-to-do shrug, hoping her blushes and glazed eyes and labored breathing weren't too noticeable. "Is this overprotective routine of Mitch's the secret of his success with women?" she asked with a tremulous laugh as she sat down to put on her boots. "Constant attention and nurturing, lots of flirtation but no actual passes, all of which make for an irresistibly intriguing combination?"

Pete slowly shook his head, looking as if he were in a daze of his own. "Not that I know of. My brother's just the opposite. He's usually too cavalier, if you ask me. I'm seeing a whole new Mitch with you, Tiffany. He didn't even fuss over his fiancée this way."

Tiffany, putting on her second boot, bolted upright, leaving the boot hanging off her toes. "Fiancée?"

"Former fiancée," Pete said hastily. "Very former. As in eight years ago. The lady took a hike right after Mitch's accident, when she found out that he might never walk again, much less have another shot at being a celebrity or getting rich from endorsements."

Accident, Tiffany thought. The skiing accident Mitch had shrugged off when she'd asked about his physiotherapy? "Never walk again?" she repeated in a small voice. "Celebrity? Endorsements?"

Pete frowned at her. "Apparently Mitch hasn't told you a whole lot about himself," he muttered.

"Apparently he hasn't," Tiffany said, quickly recovering her poise. She bent down again to pull her boot on the rest of the way. "But why should he? Being my temporary Lancelot doesn't oblige him to fill me in on his life story." Sitting up, she managed a smile. "And you needn't look so worried, Pete. I won't ask him for details."

He gave her a crooked little grin. "Not the curious type?"

"Very much the curious type," she admitted. "But I promise you, I won't try to get the rest of the story out of Mitch."

"You're an unusual woman, Tiffany."

"Thank you," she said with another smile as she got to her feet and took her handbag from a desk drawer, suffering a pang of guilt. She was curious, all right. She was putting bits of information together at computer speed, and thinking up ways to fill in the rest. "That remark, however, sounded a trifle chauvinistic," she teased, hoping Pete wasn't as tuned in to the workings of her mind as his wife and brother.

He wasn't. His grin broadened. "I suppose it did. So now that I've put both feet in my mouth, I'd better go." He turned and left, but came back a second later, ducking his head inside the door. "You're still an unusual woman," he said quietly. "And I think my brother's smart enough to know it."

Though Tiffany laughed, she was more confused than ever about Mitch. If he really was as different with her as Pete had suggested, why didn't he consider her unusual enough, or special enough, to confide in? Was she simply another conquest, more interesting than most because she was harder to get?

The memory of her fevered, abandoned response to his slightest touch made short work of that theory. She wasn't the one who was being hard to get.

Perhaps the simplest explanation was the right one. He was a midwesterner. Unlike the gregarious tourist types Tiffany was used to in Hawaii, he wasn't comfortable talking about himself.

Tiffany buttoned up her coat, tugged on her gloves, and left her office, wishing she hadn't made that rash promise to Pete not to ask Mitch for details. "I'll be a couple of hours, Cindy," she said on her way past the secretary's desk.

When Cindy didn't answer, Tiffany glanced back at her. The girl was staring off into space. "Don't get too worked up about the gorgeous Canfield men," Tiffany remarked with a deceptively bland smile. "The older one's happily married."

Cindy put on a hopeful smile. "And the younger one?"

"Spoken for," Tiffany answered firmly.

"Rats," Cindy said with a sigh. "The good ones are always taken."

Tiffany left quickly, hardly believing what she'd done—and wondering what Mitch would think if he knew she'd staked her claim on him.

TEN

By the time Mitch had turned the Jeep onto a residential street a few blocks from where he'd told her he lived, Tiffany was burning with frustrated curiosity.

Oh well, she thought philosophically. When she was with Mitch she was always burning with frustrated something. At the moment she was also burning with rage.

She was adding things up: A skiing accident that had left Mitch in bad enough shape to need a physiotherapist; a lost shot at fame and fortune; a fiancée who'd left him when he'd needed her most.

It was that thought that infuriated Tiffany and scrambled her mind so that she couldn't put all the parts together to come up with a cohesive picture. She kept dwelling on that wretch of a fiancée, wishing she could march back through time and shake some sense into the stupid woman. How anyone could be so callous was beyond her. How anyone could give up a man like Mitch when he'd cared enough to ask her to marry him was inconceivable!

No wonder he'd turned into the playboy of the western slopes.

Tiffany had to bite her tongue repeatedly to keep from betraying her promise to Pete. She was glad when Mitch pulled into a long driveway and stopped the car.

"Here's your new home away from home," he said with undisguised pride. "Unless, of course, you decide to get ornery and refuse to help out a friend in need."

Tiffany smiled. Trust Mitch to make it sound as if she would be doing someone a favor by taking the house.

It looked like an ordinary white stucco, two-story structure from the outside, nestled far back on the property amid enough trees to consitute a small forest. The setting was attractive even in the dead of winter, but Tiffany could easily picture how inviting it would be when the bare branches were covered with leaves, the house barely visible from the street.

As soon as she and Mitch went inside, Tiffany understood why Pete had suggested she jump at the place. It seemed to have been gutted and completely redesigned for an airy, open effect; its white walls and honey-colored parquet floors a perfect foil for shafts of colored light beaming in through cleverly placed stained-glass windows.

"Okay guys, she's here," Mitch called as he helped Tiffany off with her coat.

Tiffany looked around, frowning.

"The plants," Mitch said, answering her silent question. "I thought I'd better tell them that help has arrived, in case one of them is about to expire and needs only a ray of hope to keep going a little longer."

Shaking her head and laughing, Tiffany glanced past him at the group of plants that formed a room divider between the entryway and the living room. "My goodness, you aren't kidding," she commented, moving to the edge of the doormat to take a closer look. "Poor thing," she crooned as she lifted a wilting branch of a benjamina and plucked off several withered leaves. "Never mind, baby, I know what to do to make you feel better. I'll take good care of you."

"So that's how you're supposed to talk to them?" Mitch said, his voice vibrating with suppressed mirth. "I guess I was doing it all wrong."

"How *were* you doing it?" Tiffany asked, clucking over a sadly drooping spider plant. "Barking out orders for them to shape up and make it snappy?"

"Not at all," he protested in a wounded tone. "I was very friendly. Told 'em the sports scores, gave them the weather reports, that sort of thing."

Tiffany gave him a pitying look. "You're nuts. Truly crazy."

"I admit I've been one ski short of a pair lately," he said cheerfully. "Which reminds me, I took the liberty of replacing your equipment with some decent rentals I had hanging around at the shop. I think you'll notice a big difference when we go for a run this afternoon."

She spun around and stared at him. "You what?"

"I said I took the liberty of—"

"I heard you. I just can't believe it? What do you mean, you replaced my skis? What did you do with them?"

"Gave 'em to a barrelmaker in case he can use some low quality staves," Mitch said with his usual aplomb as he took off his jacket and hung it up. "The guy who sold you those things saw you coming, sweetheart. They're chipped and worn and much too long for you. Even the poles belong on the scrap heap. And before you get all riled up and start telling me how high-handed I am, close your lovely mouth for a minute and let me finish. In the first place, the rentals are on the house. In the second place, I refuse to allow you to risk a broken ankle, which is what you were doing all those times you were out practicing on your own. I'm grateful we're in flat country, or you might have taken up downhill skiing with equally lousy equipment, not to mention more determination than sense." He glanced down at her feet. "Need help with those boots?"

"No thank you," Tiffany said stiffly. She started prying them off herself, the toe of one foot holding the heel of the other in place. "What I need help with," she said after the first boot was off and she began to take off the other one, "is finding a way to get through to you that I neither want nor need your . . . your . . ." In her distracted haste, she lost her balance with her foot halfway up the calf of the boot. Stretching out her arms on both sides like a tightrope walker, she struggled to stay upright. But it was no good. She started toppling to one side.

Mitch was there to catch her, sliding one arm around her waist and steadying her against him as he leaned down and pulled her boot the rest of the way off. Straightening up, he gathered her against him. "You were saying?" he said, looking down at her with maddening, satisfied amusement.

Wrapped securely in his strong arms, Tiffany tipped back her head and tried to glare up at him, but lost the effect by bursting out laughing. The man was irresistible. She might as well forget every lecture she'd given herself since the day she'd met him. He simply demolished her defenses, no matter how carefully she constructed and reconstructed them. "You always seem to be on hand to catch me when I fall, or to put me to bed after I've dropped off to sleep, or to rescue me from some other foolishness," she said with a rueful smile. "I'm not like this, you know. I'm not clumsy as a rule, or impetuous, or even drowsy at inopportune moments. I hardly recognize myself these days."

Mitch's grin faded and his arms tightened around her. "Believe me, I know the feeling," he said quietly.

Tiffany's breath caught in her throat. Her lips instinctively parted, and her body softened against his. "Mitch," she murmured, acutely aware that they were alone and not in a hotel room. They could make love. And she wanted to. Dear heaven, she wanted to make love with this man so much, she couldn't think of anything else. "Mitch, I . . ."

He cleared his throat and reached up to curl his fingers around her wrists, lifting her hands from his chest and releasing them as he moved away from her. "I'll show you the house now," he said, his voice hoarse but his tone allowing for no argument.

She thought about throwing a boot at him, but she mustered all the bravado she could find and sashayed past him toward the living room as if she couldn't wait to see it.

She stopped in the middle of the room, her glance skimming over the thick, pearl-gray carpet and the overstuffed furniture's muted abstract upholstery. The paintings on the wall were originals by very good artists, as were several interesting carvings on the fireplace mantel. "Nice," she murmured as she heard Mitch entering the room behind her.

Folding her arms across her middle, she turned and sent him a dubious glance. "Are you sure Mr. Kozak wants a stranger living in his house? He has some beautiful things here. Why would he entrust them to someone he's never met?"

"John has my word that you'll take care of the place. Besides, everything's insured. And you can see for yourself that you're wanted. The plants are perking up already." Mitch nodded toward the doorway at the far end of the room. "C'mon. I'll give you the five-cent tour."

Tiffany followed, making properly appreciative remarks as she viewed the quietly elegant home. But the seed of an unpleasant suspicion had taken root in her mind. Why wouldn't Mitch make love to her? Was he a truly dangerous Don Juan, the kind whose ego demanded emotional conquests as well as physical ones, who wasn't satisfied until he'd won a woman's whole heart and soul, who had to make sure she would never forget him once he moved on?

She couldn't accept the idea. Not Mitch, she thought. Mitch was too much his own man to need to affirm his own sense of self-worth by destroying someone else's.

But she'd fallen into that trap once before, she reminded herself. It might be wise to allow for the possibility that it was happening again. "This is a wonderful house," she said crisply. "I'd love to stay here. Now, let's talk rent."

The rent argument went on through a pirogi-and-salad lunch at a tiny Ukrainian restaurant. Mitch claimed that his friend was grateful to have a plant-sitter and wouldn't accept a penny, while Tiffany flatly refused to move in unless she paid something. She wouldn't budge on the issue. She didn't want to feel any more obliged to Mitch than she already did.

They compromised. She could pay for the heat and utilities while she stayed in the house.

With that discussion out of the way, Mitch gave her a duplicate set of keys he'd already had made for her from the ones his friend had given him.

After lunch, he insisted on taking her back to the

hotel to pack up her things and move to the house immediately. "What's the hurry?" she protested. "It's too late for me to check out today anyway."

"That's no reason for you to stay there another night when the house is available," Mitch countered. "And it won't take long to move you, so let's do it."

By one-thirty, Tiffany had taken up residence in her new home.

"Now, I have to head down to the store to work with a sales rep from one of my suppliers," Mitch said as Tiffany climbed out of the Cherokee after he'd driven her back to the packaging plant. "Usually the guy wants to go out for dinner after we've finished putting an order together, but I can get out of it so you and I can do takeout or something. I'll try to finish by four and pick you up for a skiing session."

Tiffany bent down to peer into the Jeep at him with a slight frown. "You seem to have everything all worked out. Does it occur to you that I might have plans of my own? Different plans?"

He lifted one brow. "Do you?"

"Well no, but . . ."

"Then there's no problem," he said with a grin and a wink.

Rolling her eyes, Tiffany gave him a smart salute and closed the door.

By two-thirty, she'd caught up on all the reports and summaries she could do for the time being, so she slipped out of the office and headed for a nearby library she'd noticed that morning on the way to work.

She'd promised Pete she wouldn't quiz Mitch, but she hadn't said anything about not using her well-developed research skills to satisfy her curiosity.

Two hours later, she was still at the library, finding out what a total stranger Mitch Canfield was to her—and wondering why he was so closemouthed about parts of his life any normal man would be proud of.

She could think of only one reason. After all these years, he was still carrying a torch for that long-gone fiancée.

Mitch called Tiffany just before four to tell her he was running late and to apologize for being unable to take her skiing after all. To his mild surprise, she wasn't there. "Ms. Greer stepped out for a while," the secretary said in a breathy little voice. "Is there anything *I* can do for you, Mr. Canfield?"

Mitch frowned at the receiver. The young lady sounded as if she should be at the other end of a nine hundred number. "Perhaps you could give Ms. Greer a message," he said with exaggerated formality. "Please tell her I'm tied up looking at a new line of sports goods, but should be finished around six. I'll check in with her then."

The apology would have to wait, he thought as he hung up, his message duly recorded and read back to him.

As soon as he arrived home at six, he phoned Tiffany at the Kozak house. He smiled at the mere sound of her voice when she answered, but his smile faded as he sensed an uncharacteristic hesitance in her tone, and he was scowling by the time he hung up. He'd apologized for being delayed, especially since he'd made it impossible for her to go skiing without him, and she hadn't seemed to have minded missing the outing. "I'm too tired anyway," she'd said. "I've been pushing hard on all fronts lately. Maybe it's caught up with me. I have the makings for a tuna sandwich, so I think I'll eat that and then go straight to bed."

Okay, Mitch thought. She probably did need a quiet night. Or perhaps this was her way of telling him he was being pushy. But Tiffany? Hell, she'd come right out with a straightforward, "Back off," or words to that effect.

Something about her kept nagging at him. She'd thanked him too profusely for arranging for her to have the house. She'd brought up the rent argument again, saying she'd feel better if she could keep everything on a businesslike basis.

A businesslike basis, he brooded as he rummaged through the freezer for something to heat up in the microwave. Weren't he and Tiffany a long way past that stage?

He found a macaroni dinner, nuked it, and spent the evening in front of the television, watching sitcoms that weren't funny.

It was the next afternoon, when he called Tiffany at the office to ask about skiing and dinner, that his stomach really began twisting into a knot.

It turned out that she'd agreed to go to the ballet with some of the women from the office, and couldn't even take time for an hour of skiing. Fine, he told himself. She had a right to a life of her own. And she'd sounded honestly regretful when she'd turned him down.

But he sensed that she was pulling back, distancing herself from him, and he had no idea why.

He began questioning himself. He didn't know how long Tiffany would be in Winnipeg. In a race against time, was he running in the wrong direction? Was he being too cautious, trying to win her heart without binding her to him right away with physical intimacy?

He'd been conscious all along of a deep wariness in her, a cache of fears that had been formed during her parents' unhappy marriage and confirmed, he was certain, by some bastard who'd abused her trust. It would take patience and time to overcome those fears. Patience had been his strong suit ever since he'd learned the hard way what the cost of impatience could be. But whether or not he had enough time seemed to be up to Paradise Foods.

And now, for reasons he couldn't fathom, Tiffany was slipping away from him.

That evening, as he downed a tasteless take-out hamburger while standing at his kitchen counter, he made up his mind. He was no good at guessing games. He was going to confront Tiffany in the morning. He would go to her office, lock the door, and get the truth out of her one way or the other.

He immediately felt better. Waiting for what he wanted wasn't his style. He preferred to fight. And if fighting for Tiffany meant hauling her into his arms and keeping her there until he had some answers, so much the better.

In fact, he just might keep her there after he got his answers as well.

It was nearly midnight when Tiffany arrived home after her evening at the ballet. She'd gone out for drinks with the others, putting off being alone as long as possible. Being alone meant agonizing over Mitch, wondering whether she was being a fool, wondering whether she was being a coward. No. *Knowing* she was being a coward. She was running scared. She didn't like herself very much at the moment, but she'd guarded her heart for as long as she could remember, even against her own parents. It wasn't an easy habit to break. The one time she'd lowered her shield, she'd been knocked silly. She'd chosen the worst kind of man to trust.

She supposed trust was like anything else, though. It took practice to get it right.

She thought about calling Mitch, if only to be honest with him, to tell him why she'd been shying away. Didn't she owe him a proper explanation? Didn't she owe it to herself to do battle with the stubborn memory of his fiancée? Wasn't it better to risk losing than not to fight at all?

In the morning, she decided. She would phone him first thing in the morning.

Feeling better, yet a little shaky at the prospect of taking emotional risks when she was much better at backing down from them, she paid the cabdriver and searched for her keys as she hurried up the front walk. It was a frigid night, and she didn't have enough layers under her coat to keep her warm. Her daffodil coat, she thought with a tiny smile. Mitch would give her proper hell if he knew she hadn't bundled up properly.

She scowled as she realized that she hadn't put the porch light on when she'd left the house earlier. Her confusion about Mitch had spilled over into every aspect of her life and turned her into an absentminded dolt.

Finally locating the key chain by touch at the bottom of her purse, she pulled it out, her hand trembling. To her horror, it slipped from her fingers and fell into the deep snow that had drifted around a cluster of dwarf evergreens next to the front steps. "Oh no," she said softly. "Now you've really done it!" She looked back at the street. The cab was gone. She had to find the keys.

She tried staying on the shoveled walk and reaching over to pat carefully around the spot where she thought the keys might be, though she hadn't seen them land. Nothing.

She had no choice but to leave the walk and plow

through the snow to search more closely. She was wearing her black knee-high boots with socks inside them, but within moments her legs felt as if they were encased in ice, the unlined patent leather trapping the cold.

Trying not to panic, she searched the snow around the trees, looking for a hole in the glittering white surface. There were several. They all looked as if they could be harboring a set of keys, but she found only branches and fallen icicles in them.

After scrabbling around in vain until her hands were numb, Tiffany gave up the search and returned to the walk. She looked up and down the street. Not a single light was on in any of the houses. Evidently she was in an early-to-bed neighborhood. Besides, she didn't know a soul. A cold climate didn't lend itself to chit-chats over the back fence.

Mitch, she thought. Mitch had another set of keys. And he lived only a few blocks away. He'd pointed out his house once when they'd driven past it on their way downtown.

Tiffany groaned. *Only* a few blocks? She was freezing already, and she wasn't sure she knew the way. If she could find the right street—and thank heavens, he'd mentioned the name and she remembered it—she might spot the red Cherokee.

Unless it was in a garage.

Unless he wasn't home.

Unless he'd given up on her and was spending the

night with a woman who wasn't riddled with stupid hang-ups.

She started out, hoping that by moving fast enough she could maintain enough body warmth to keep going until she found Mitch's house, a telephone booth, or a passing taxi.

ELEVEN

Mitch had just undressed for bed when he heard the faint rapping on his front door. The sound was so weak, he'd have missed it if some sixth sense hadn't put him on the alert.

His stomach clenched and the hairs on the back of his neck rose. There wasn't the slightest doubt in his mind who was at the door, though he couldn't have explained how he knew.

Throwing on a robe, he raced downstairs, and yanked open the door without looking through the peephole. "My God," he exploded, dragging Tiffany inside. He pushed the door shut and enfolded her in his arms.

"I lost my keys," she said, her voice so tiny, it was almost inaudible. "In the snow."

Mitch cursed. "I should be shot. Why didn't I give you an extra set? It's so damned easy to drop them and so hard to find them again. I can't believe I overlooked something so basic."

"I could have had an extra set made myself, but I didn't get around to it," she protested as she burrowed into him, seeking his warmth. "Besides, I wouldn't be so cold if I'd taken your advice about buying a better dress coat and lined boots. The whole mess is my own fault. And you're here to rescue me again. I wasn't sure you would be, but you always are."

Mitch tightened his arms around her slender, shaking body, still blaming himself. He should have bought a coat for her when she was too stubborn to do it herself. He should have spent more time explaining all the things that could happen. He should have made sure she had extra keys.

But the only thing that counted was getting Tiffany warm. She was scrunched up, pressing herself so close to him, she was practically inside his robe. Amazingly, though she was like a block of ice against his bare skin, he hardly noticed the cold. His body seemed intent only on cranking up its own temperature to pour heat into hers.

What she needed, however, was something more than a warm cuddle. Lifting her in his arms, he carried her upstairs to the bathroom where he gently set her down to stand beside the large tub. "The quickest way to get you fixed up is in a bath," he said as she snuggled insistently against him, reluctant to let him go even long enough for him to turn on the taps and reach over to the light switches to flick on the overhead heat lamp.

"We'll start with lukewarm and gradually heat it up," he said, somehow managing to get the water running while holding on to her. He kept her in his arms for a few moments, hating to release her as much as she resisted it. "Honey, we have to get you out of your clothes," he said at last. "Starting with your boots."

"Stupid boots," she said through chattering teeth as she let him sit her down on a small stool next to the tub and start easing off the stiff boots. "No. Stupid me. I was never cold in the Sorels, or in any of the things you picked out for me. Only in my dressy clothes, and you warned me a thousand times that they weren't warm enough." Tears suddenly appeared in her eyes. "Why didn't I listen to you, when you'd proven time and time again that you knew what you were talking about?"

Setting her boots aside and pulling Tiffany to her feet, Mitch's lips quirked in a suppressed grin. She was going to hate herself in the morning for all this self-recrimination. "Maybe I wasn't diplomatic enough," he suggested magnanimously, struggling to remove her coat while she battled to crawl back inside his robe.

Tiffany rubbed her cold nose against a warm, furry spot in the middle of his chest. "You weren't diplomatic at all. But that's no excuse. I should have taken every bit of advice you ever tried to give me."

He couldn't hold back a low chuckle. "Well, sweetheart, you'll have plenty of time to make up for being so difficult. I'm sure I'll give you all kinds of advice in the future, and you can atone for the past by following it without a whisper of argument."

Since Tiffany was certain she'd do anything Mitch told her to do if only he'd keep holding her, keeping her safe in his strong arms and warmed by the heat radiating from his every pore, she nodded. "Not a whisper," she vowed.

After all the times Mitch had buttoned and unbuttoned her coat, zipped and unzipped her jacket, bundled her into extra sweaters and tucked scarves around her neck, it seemed perfectly natural to Tiffany to cooperate while he undressed her. Actually, it seemed very nice. Lovely. She hadn't planned this situation deliberately, but if she'd thought of it, she might have given it a try. Freezing half to death was a small price to pay for this bliss.

She helped a little with the process of getting rid of her clothes, but Mitch was so capable, he didn't need much assistance. She was free to warm her hands on his chest and rub each newly exposed inch of her skin against him.

"At least you were wearing reasonably heavy tights," he said as he smoothly stripped them off.

Tiffany lifted one foot and ran her bare toes along the inside of his calf. "Only because opaque tights are in style," she admitted, raising her other foot and warming it the same way. "I've been an obstinate twit."

Mitch was beginning to respond in a normal but untimely way to Tiffany's efforts to warm her various body parts. "I'll see if I can find a hair shirt and some ashes for you," he muttered as he unhooked her bra and slid the straps off her shoulders and down her arms.

Tiffany tipped back her head and frowned up at him. "You'll find what?"

"Nothing." He tossed her bra aside and battled to maintain some level of clinical objectivity, even when Tiffany melted against him, her soft breasts tipped by rigid little nubs that made his blood simmer dangerously. He knew it was the cold that had hardened her nipples, but he couldn't stop thinking about an enjoyable way to warm them.

Swallowing hard, he hooked his thumbs under the waistband of her panties, took a deep breath, and tugged them down.

Fully naked, she was lovely beyond his dreams, her breasts high and firm, her narrow waist tapering out to a graceful flare of hip. Her skin was soft and creamy, burnished to a peachy gold glow, the peaks of her breasts the same dusky pink as her lips.

Mitch's mouth ached to taste the sweetness of her, but as he smoothed his hands over her long, graceful back and the gentle roundness of her bottom, he felt how cold she still was. His robe was open, so he wrapped it around her, cradling her against him while the tub finished filling.

When there was finally enough water to climb into, Mitch turned off the taps and twisted the dial to activate the whirlpool jets. Tiffany curled her arms around his neck and moved with him as if they were locked in some strange, intimate dance.

He could see only one solution. Sweeping her up in his arms again, he carefully stepped into the deep tub and lowered them both into the gushing, swirling water, cradling her in his lap.

"This is so nice," she murmured, her lips grazing the hollow above his collarbone. "Does every house in Winnipeg have a Jacuzzi?"

Mitch laughed quietly. "Of course. And under the snow, all the streets are paved with gold."

"I'm so glad," she said with a sigh. "I thought it was just more snow." Relaxing against him, she closed her eyes, her long lashes fluttering over his skin like a tantalizing kiss.

It took every ounce of his self-control simply to hold her when his body was demanding so much more. If someone had told him weeks before that he would care enough for any woman to draw on all his reserves of self-discipline to resist having her, he'd have laughed off the idea as pure nonsense.

Yet here he was, cuddling his sweet Tiffany, stroking her arm, savoring the heady bouquet of her womanly scent, lapping water over the curve of her shoulder and the slopes of her breasts, and mentally reciting multiplication tables.

As the water cooled, he had to shift to reach the taps to warm it up. He regretted each time he had to disturb Tiffany, but it was necessary. "Sorry," he said after the third warm-up, when the bath was hot enough for steam to rise from it.

She tipped back her head to smile drowsily up at

him. "Don't be sorry. This is lovely. And it works. I'm warm all the way through."

"Good. We'll stay a little longer, then get you off to bed."

Tiffany smiled again, then nuzzled her face into the curve of his neck. A moment later, she began pressing soft kisses to his throat and shoulders and chest, her fingers trailing over his thigh.

Mitch caught his breath, beginning to see stars. He managed to say lightly, "Am I being seduced, by any chance?"

"I don't know," Tiffany said, taking tiny, kittenlike licks at his skin with the tip of her tongue. "Are you?"

He answered by letting his hand glide over her hip and waist to her midriff, then her breast, cupping one rose-tipped mound in his palm as he dipped his head and sought her mouth. "I think I'm starting to catch on," he murmured, nibbling on her full lower lip. "You'll go to any lengths to get me into bed."

Knowing he was teasing, Tiffany laughed and ran her fingers through the wet coils of hair on his chest, her nails gently scratchy. "The situation had become impossible. I had to take drastic action." Her tongue met his and danced a bit. Then, with another smile that was both innocent and sultry, she asked softly, "Is it going to do me any good?"

Mitch gazed at her, imprinting the moment on his mind for permanent safekeeping, then answered by capturing her mouth in a long, leisurely kiss that was an erotic promise. His hands moved over her, shaping her curves, learning her contours as if she were a priceless treasure that had come into his possession by some unexplained miracle.

"You do want me," Tiffany whispered as her palm, resting on the middle of his chest, felt the wild throbbing of his heart. "You really do."

"My God, Tiffany," he said, his voice thick with desire. He took her hand in his and moved it downward until she was touching the irrefutable evidence of his need. "Yes, I want you. I've told you how much. Time and again you've seen and felt how much I want you. Surely you've never had doubts about that."

As she lightly stroked the rigid, silky length of him, her breasts rose and fell with her shallow, ragged breathing. "I haven't any doubts now, Mitch. None at all."

He placed her arms around his neck, then spanned her waist with his hands and lifted her with him as he got to his feet and stepped out of the tub. Wrapping her in his own thick terry-cloth robe, he rained gentle kisses over her upturned face and spoke softly, caressingly. "At some point, my sweet darling, I'll make love to you in this tub. And in the shower, and probably under the dining room table. Anywhere and everywhere that we can be alone and uninhibited. But right now I want you where I've wanted you all along. Not in a hotel room, not at the farm, and not in some other man's bed, even if it's yours temporarily. You belong in my bed, Tiffany Greer, and that's where you're about to find yourself." He smiled and pushed back a few damp tendrils of her hair. "Are you going to give me an argument on this one?"

With her eyes shining and her lips curved in a smile that was the epitome of feminine mystery, Tiffany slowly wagged her head from side to side.

Mitch's pulse raced crazily. His heart was expanding in his chest, threatening to burst. His hands were shaking as his body urged him to hurry, to carry Tiffany to his bed and plunge into her soft, moist warmth.

Yet he forced himself to advance slowly, to draw out this first lovemaking with Tiffany to its furthest limits.

He sat her down on the stool after pulling it out from beside the tub and placing it in front of the vanity, and began drying her dampened hair.

She watched him in the mirror for a while, following his every move as if mesmerized. He thought about slinging a towel around his middle, but he liked the way her heavy-lidded eyes devoured him. Then she turned to face him directly, and her gaze was so searing, it made the heat lamp seem cool.

He'd finished drying her hair when she started touching him, but Mitch didn't rush to move away. She reached up to tunnel the fingertips of both hands through the coarse, springy coils of his chest hair, then slid her palms outward in wide, sweeping motions that fanned out in opposite directions and gradually spiraled smaller and smaller, finally tracing the brown aureoles around his nipples. When she flicked her thumbs over the hard nubs, heat crackled through him like lines of electricity connected directly to the very core of his being.

He carefully put down the dryer and laced his fingers through the blue-black silk of her hair, tentatively drawing her toward him until her lips were pressed directly over his pounding heart. Her tongue fluttered against his skin and her hands followed a slow, downward path to his hips and flanks and the creases of his thighs. Somewhere in the recesses of his mind he recalled that he'd meant to stay in control, orchestrate every shared delight. Instead, she'd taken the reins. He was supposed to be pleasuring her, but she was pleasuring him. And dear lord, *how* she was pleasuring him. Her lips and tongue created magic, and her hands were as light and teasing as the thrumming wings of a hummingbird. "You're so beautiful," she whispered, her breath warm on his skin. "It's so good to be able to touch you this way. And to taste you . . ."

A harsh groan tore from Mitch's throat. She'd brought him to the edge of a precipice, and he had to stop her before he went over it. Dropping his hands to her shoulders, he raised her up and pulled her against him, lowered his lips to hers, and took her mouth in a wild, ravaging kiss.

Seconds later she was naked again, the robe pooled at her feet. Her arms were around his neck, her body molded to his. "You feel so good," he whispered, his hands moving down her spine to the base, then flaring out to cup her bottom. "I've wanted to have you against me this way for so long, sweetheart. Is it really happening?"

"I think so. And it could have happened sooner," she scolded lovingly as she nibbled at his lower lip. "Why didn't it, Mitch? Why did you pull away from me when you knew how much I wanted you?"

"I think I had a good reason," he answered, his fingers tightening on her soft flesh. He thrust her lower body hard against him to banish any lingering question of whether he intended to pull away this time. "But for the life of me, sweetheart, I can't remember it right now."

She moved her hips in a tantalizing circle that nearly sent him through the ceiling. "Don't remember it," she urged him. "Don't even try."

He was hardly aware of scooping her up in his arms, or of carrying her to the bedroom, but suddenly they were there, and he was lowering her to the mattress, his body stretched full length over hers.

Every fiber of his being was clamoring for release, but his determination was even stronger than his need. He trailed lingering kisses over her face, her throat, her shoulders, down the inside of each arm to her fingertips. His tongue teased her palms, the throbbing pulse spot of her wrists, the inner crooks of her elbows. His lips and tongue gave untiring attention to her breasts before moving over her midriff and stomach.

"I can't bear it," Tiffany cried. "Mitch, *please*, I can't wait . . ."

"You can," he said quietly. "Have patience, love. The journey's as rewarding as the goal."

With a shuddering sigh, Tiffany gave herself to the sweet journey, with Mitch as her guide.

It was a long, slow voyage of discovery, full of delicious shocks and beautiful surprises. She'd had no idea how sensually alive she was, how many ways she could be caressed to undreamed-of heights, how many places on her body were like touch-sensitive keys to a whole new erotic world, a world where nothing existed but what Mitch was doing, what Mitch was making her feel. His thumb delicately traced the arch of her foot. His lips grazed along the inside of her calf from ankle to knee. His whiskery cheek rubbed over her thighs and belly. She heard herself whimpering as his tongue swirled tiny circles along the underside of her rib cage, the inner softness of her arms. He gently kneaded and squeezed her breasts, drew their tips between his teeth and soothed them with his tongue.

She was on fire. Every particle, every cell was in flames as Mitch moved up beside her, cradled her against him, and captured her lips in a kiss of excruciating tenderness. His free hand moved over her, barely touching her skin yet triggering a jolt of pure sensual energy in every nerve ending. He touched the spot that was the electrified center of her need, and met her cries with deep thrusts of his tongue into the recesses of her mouth. As his fingers began exploring her most intimate secrets, she felt the petals of her femininity unfurling like a tight hibiscus bud opening to the sun.

"Mitch," she gasped. "Dear heaven, Mitch, now, please now . . ."

"Yes. Yes, baby. Yes. Now." He moved over her and slowly, slowly eased himself into her warmth and closed his lips over hers. Her mouth softened. She loosened her grip on his shoulders and twined her arms around his neck. Her body seemed to melt, sweetly luring him, drawing him into her irresistible softness.

Her surrender conquered him. With a groan, he plunged deeply into her. They began moving in an ancient rhythm, floating on gently undulating waves that steadily grew more powerful.

"Mitch?" Tiffany whispered, gripped by an unfamiliar sensation that startled her, a strange feeling of not knowing where she left off and he began. "Mitch, hold me!" she cried, as if she might shatter without him to keep her together.

He slid both arms under her and crushed her against him. "I've got you, sweetheart. I won't let go."

All at once the world stopped. Time stopped. Tiffany felt a column of intense, explosive heat rising inside her. She looked up at Mitch, making his eyes a focal point in a universe that was starting to whirl out of control.

"Let it happen," he said. "Don't fight it, love." His eyes darkened. Every muscle in his body was taut. His hands slid down to cup her bottom and lift her to him as his breath turned to harsh gasps.

Suddenly a thousand sensations swept over Tiffany and the heat inside her erupted like an overflowing geyser. Mitch was pounding wildly into her with shouts of primitive male triumph that mingled with her own helpless, keening wail.

At that moment, there wasn't a fear in the world that could touch her. Seeking Mitch's mouth in a kiss to complete the circle of their union, she knew only perfect, glorious nirvana.

With Tiffany nestled in the crook of his arm, the blankets tucked snugly around her, Mitch smiled contentedly. "I remember now why I wanted to wait until the time was right for us to make love," he said quietly.

"Mmm?" Tiffany responded, pressing her lips to his shoulder.

"Fortunately," he said with a quiet laugh, "the time was perfect tonight."

She merely sighed and shifted a little, flinging one arm over his middle and one leg over his thighs.

"I didn't—and don't— want an affair with you," he went on, absently stroking her shoulder. "I mean, not *just* an affair." He dropped a light kiss on the top of her head, took a deep breath that filled his nostrils with her sweet feminine scent, and forged ahead with sudden determination. "I know there are details to be worked out between us, questions we both want to ask, compromises to be reached. But the main issue is settled. We belong to each other. You're mine, sweetheart. All mine. Whether you fully understand it or not, you belong to me now, as I belong to you—and probably have since that first day at the airport." He smiled again and cuddled her a little closer, pleased that she wasn't protesting. "And by God," he added since he seemed to be on a roll, "whatever other ideas you still might be entertaining, I intend to keep you, whatever it takes."

Wincing slightly at what might be a touch of over-confidence on his part, he braced himself to hear Tiffany suggest he was awfully arrogant if he thought she would stay in a godforsaken, frigid country thousands of miles from her home, not for a few months or even a year or two, but indefinitely. He would explain, of course, that he was prepared to go back to Hawaii with her if she wanted it that way. Life had taught him flexibility.

She didn't utter a word.

A suspicion crept into Mitch's mind. He cocked his head to one side so he could see Tiffany's face.

Her lips were curved in a dreamy smile. Her eyes were closed, her long lashes dark against her love-flushed cheeks. Her breathing was deep and regular.

Mitch laughed quietly and reached for the light switch by his side of the bed. He doubted if she'd heard anything he'd said. Maybe it was just as well.

Patience, he told himself. Patience was always the key.

TWELVE

"Do you think it's time you told me what happened after I left you at the house the day before yesterday?" Mitch asked casually as he cupped his hand under Tiffany's elbow to propel her into a downtown department store.

"Not much," Tiffany answered. Feigning innocence, she tried to fend off the question by continuing hastily, "I heard from Honolulu. It seems our CEO has been tied up with some other big project, but he'll get to the decision on this one very soon. On the home front, Mr. Kozak's benjamina is feeling better, and the other plants will be happy campers soon."

Checking the store directory, Mitch found what he was looking for. "Women's coats, third floor," he said, then turned to Tiffany with a patient smile as he steered her toward the escalators. "Now, honeybunch, drop the act. You know what I was asking. When I left you two days ago, everything was hunky-dory between us. When I called you that night, you started playing hide-and-seek, and kept it up until your subconscious took over and threw your keys into the snow to force you to come to me. What was it all about?"

Tiffany's eyes widened. "My . . . my . . . my subconscious did what?" she sputtered.

He threw back his head and laughed. "Gotcha! It's good to have the old Tiffany back. Sweetheart, I was *kidding*." Abruptly turning thoughtful, he said, "Still, you have to admit that it's an interesting theory."

"I don't have to admit any such thing! Losing those keys was an accident. Even you said it happens all the time. And since you're going to pester me for an explanation until you get one, here it is. The reason I was a little . . . well, rattled, was that I . . . I . . . " She frowned, her mind suddenly a blank. How could she make Mitch understand the panic that had taken control of her when she hardly understood it herself?

Staring at him while he waited for her to finish, Tiffany stiffened her spine and decided to confess. "After you left to meet that salesman of yours, I went to the library and found out a few things about you that disturbed me."

Mitch cocked one brow, grinning. "Sounds serious. But I'm puzzled. What could you have found out that's worse than what you already believed?"

"You were an Olympic skier," she said as they stepped onto the escalator. "An *Olympic* skier!"

"Oh, well, no wonder you were upset. That's heavy

stuff. If you'd discovered that I'm a bigamist and a mob hit man, it wouldn't have been so bad. But an Olympic skier? Who could blame you for running scared?"

Tiffany refused to rise to his bait. "I also know about your subsequent career as a ski instructor in some of the most exclusive resorts in Europe. You've hob-nobbed with the Robin Leach crowd. You've squired women I've read about in the social columns of *Vogue* and *Town And Country*. You've given schussing point-ers to *royalty*!"

He shook his head and laughed. "Yeah, so?"

"So you never told me!"

"It was years ago. Should I have introduced myself to you as Mitch Canfield, one-time Olympic hopeful? Former mascot to the idle rich?"

"Don't talk that way. Why do you insist on present-ing yourself in the worst possible light? For a while I thought it was because you wanted to make sure no woman with half a brain would get interested in you for more than a fling. . . ."

"Really?" he asked with a quizzical smile, taking her arm as they left the escalator. "Interesting. Could be, I suppose, though the thought never occurred to me." He looked around, spotted the coats, and started toward them. "We might as well get all the ancient history out of the way. I guess you also know that the accident I mentioned was a case of literally bending myself out of shape trying to win a gold medal?"

"I read about your accident, yes. About how you lost the gold because of it, but won the more important prize of learning to walk again—and ski again—despite the odds. These things are important, Mitch. Why wouldn't you have mentioned them, especially when I asked you about your accident? Why did you always manage to avoid giving me a straight answer?"

He stopped at a rack of heavy wool coats and riffled through them. "I could say that it was all such a long time ago, I rarely think about it," he said with a careless shrug. "I could claim that it brings back too much pain. But the truth is, I have no particular desire to talk about things that embarrass me."

"Embarrass you? You made it to the Olympics, lost out on the gold only because of an accident, recovered completely despite a grim prognosis, and you're embarrassed?"

"It wasn't an accident. It was stupidity." He pulled a royal-blue coat off the rack and held it up to take a closer look at it. "I wanted that gold too much. I was a young hotshot, convinced I knew more than my coach did. I ignored his advice, pushed too hard before I was ready, and wiped out."

"And that's something to be embarrassed about? You're awfully hard on yourself," Tiffany commented.

Mitch put the blue coat back, muttering that it was too heavy for her. "It wouldn't have been so bad if I'd been the only person affected, but I let others down. The team, the sponsors, the coaches—the whole damn country, for that matter. It takes years, money, and a lot of dedicated people to get one athlete onto an Olympic team, let alone all the way to a podium. I blew it all in a few seconds of defiance because I thought silver wasn't good enough for me. The best I can say for the whole experience is that I got some priorities straightened out, learned to live in the present instead of dwelling on some single, elusive moment of glory, and lost a fiancée I'd been engaged to for all the wrong reasons."

"You were bitter about her. That woman's defection has colored your whole existence ever since, your relationships with all women," Tiffany said, finally getting down to what really bothered her.

"I beg your pardon?" He stared at her with a shocked smile.

"You heard me."

He turned to a rack of down-filled coats, pulled out three in her size, grabbed her hand, and hauled her off to the fitting room.

"You can't come in here," Tiffany said as he led her into one of the stalls and closed the door behind them.

"We're alone. I checked," he said. "No feet showing under the doors."

"But someone—"

"Tiffany, listen to me," he cut in, hanging the coats on a hook. "I want to straighten you out right now. That fiancée left me a bitter young man, yes. For about two months, maybe even three. But by the time I was back on my feet, I'd realized what a narrow escape I'd had. She was pretty. She could be charming when she chose. But she wasn't for me. That wipeout cost me a gold medal, but it got me a reprieve from a terrible mistake. Since that time, I've never been deeply involved. I've occasionally wondered why. I put it down to basic emotional laziness, but now I know better." He cradled Tiffany's face in his hands and gave her a long, lingering kiss, then said softly, "The reason was simple, sweetheart. I hadn't met you."

Tiffany's eyes filled with tears. "Oh Mitch," she murmured.

He smiled. "I love the way you say that. Again, sweetheart. Say it again."

"Oh Mitch," she said, throwing her arms around him.

He held her close for a long while, then finally ordered in a thick, hoarse voice, "Okay, you. Try on these things right now. We don't leave here until you've got a warm coat to wear."

Tiffany smiled. Intense emotion made the man so adorably dictatorial.

Buying more winter clothes so late in the season had seemed like a foolish extravagance to Tiffany, but when she hadn't seen the slightest sign of spring by the end of the first week of March, she was glad to have the cozy lightweight green coat Mitch had helped her choose, as well as the lined knee-high boots that kept her toes warm without extra socks.

On Friday morning, she found a fax on her desk, sent from Honolulu at the end of the business day there and well before morning in Winnipeg. The long-awaited decision from headquarters had arrived. The terms she'd negotiated with the Canfields were acceptable to Paradise Foods. A lawyer would be on the way within days to make the deal official.

Tiffany was delighted by the news.

Then she read the last paragraph of the message. It was like a kick in the stomach. She read it again. "That's not fair," she whispered. "It's rotten, miserable, stinking *unfair*!"

After a few minutes of absorbing the shock, she reached for the phone to call Mitch, but her hand hovered over the receiver. They had plans for a special weekend. Why ruin it?

Early in the week, Pete and Jackie had packed up the children and headed south, and wouldn't be back until late Sunday night. They'd asked Mitch to look in on the farm and pick up their mail. He, in turn, had come up with a plan Tiffany had loved. "What do you say we protect the place properly by staying right there from Friday night to, say, early Sunday evening?" he'd suggested. "We'd be doing the family a favor. They left their van at the airport carpark, so I don't have to meet their plane. They'll be thrilled to come back to a warm house, and we'll be able to spend the weekend enjoying some *real* cross-country skiing—no crowding, no noise, no cranked-up ghetto blasters. Just the two of us breaking our own trails in the snow."

She'd decided to take Friday afternoon off to add a few precious extra hours to their little getaway.

She made a snap decision. Her news—the good and

the bad—could wait until Sunday night. Nothing was going to spoil this weekend with Mitch.

It could very well be their last.

By eleven-thirty, she was a mass of excitement and nerves, trying not to think beyond the next two days as she waited impatiently for Mitch to pick her up at the Kozak house for a late lunch at the farm.

As soon as she saw the Cherokee pull up, she threw on her coat and boots and was ready to go by the time Mitch knocked on the door. "Sorry I took so long," he said, his hair even more rumpled than usual. "I had a few errands to run that took me longer than I expected." He grinned as his glance slid over her. "You seem to be all set to go."

"I am," she said, picking up the overnight bag she'd packed when she'd stopped off at her place early in the morning to dress for work. Mitch always smiled sardonically at this ritual but didn't complain about it. He seemed to understand that she needed to cling to her autonomy. "You've brought my other things?" she asked. She kept her equipment and ski togs at his house.

Mitch clapped his hand to his forehead. "I knew I'd forgotten something!"

She believed him for about five seconds, until she saw the mischievous light in his eyes. "Okay, okay, I didn't need to ask," she said, giving his shoulder a mock punch. "Sorry. I'm a compulsive checker, probably because I'm not used to being able to depend on someone else."

"Get used to it," he said sternly, tucking her hand under his arm, then relented with a smile and a wink. "But it doesn't hurt to check. Even I'm not infallible, believe it or not."

Get used to it, she repeated silently. She only wished she would have the chance.

"Tiffany?" Mitch said, reaching out to crook his finger under her chin to make her look up at him. "Is something bothering you?"

She forced a smile. "Yes. That last remark of yours begged for a comeback, and I can't think of one."

He laughed, accepting her answer at face value.

The drive to the farm was pleasant. Mitch had heard from Pete that morning and was armed with amusing stories about the great time the family was having, so Tiffany didn't have to struggle to maintain an upbeat conversation.

As soon as they arrived, Mitch asked, "Are you starved, or are you game for a little skiing to work up an appetite?"

"Let's strap on the boards," Tiffany answered, delighting in Mitch's groan of mock exasperation at her cornball jargon.

A few minutes later they were gliding across the pristine fields. "What a beautiful day," Tiffany said, breathing in the clean, crisp air. "I can't believe how warm it is."

Mitch grinned. "Almost zero. Balmy, remember?"

Since there was no need for ski masks on such a mild day, Mitch had made sure her face was well slathered with sunblock, her lips with protective balm. She'd had to shut her eyes as he'd fussed over her. Tears, perilously close to the surface, had threatened to spill over. She was going to miss his protectiveness. She was going to miss his smile, his teasing, his bossy ways. Dear heaven, she was going to miss so much about him.

They were approaching a familiar grove of trees before Tiffany realized that Mitch was leading her to his tree house.

They took off their skis and climbed up to it, and the moment she ducked through the low doorway of the hut, Tiffany burst into tears. A thick, inviting sleeping bag was laid out on an air mattress on the floor. Beside it were a portable heater, a picnic basket filled to overflowing, and a bottle of Dom Pérignon nestled into a silver ice bucket.

Mitch took off his gloves and undid his jacket zipper, then gathered her into his arms. "Hey, I wanted to make you happy."

"You did," she said, wrapping her arms around his waist and holding him as if determined never to let him go. "You always do. You turn every moment into a . . . a celebration. Oh Mitch, I love you." She caught her breath, horrified by what she'd blurted out. Her timing was appalling. What was he supposed to do now? Dutifully return the sentiment? Try to explain that he was extremely fond of her, but love wasn't on the agenda?

He cupped her chin and made her look up at him. "I

was hoping you'd get around to that confession sooner or later," he said quietly, searching her eyes. "Because I love you too."

Tiffany stared at him, her heart pounding. He loved her? Was it possible? Did he mean it, or was it just a glib phrase? No! Not Mitch. He'd never be careless with those words.

She almost told him then that she'd been summoned back to Hawaii and had to leave in a few days. But she couldn't. Not at that moment. It would be like presenting him with an ultimatum: Did he love her enough to ask her not to go?

If he didn't, she preferred not to know yet.

And if he did, was she ready to give up everything to stay?

She preferred not to deal with that question yet, either.

"Honey, are you sure everything's okay?" he asked gently.

Tiffany slowly shook her head and reached up to curl her arms around his neck. "I'm too stunned to talk, that's all." She smiled seductively. "Can you think of something else to do?"

He searched her eyes for a long moment, then lowered his head and barely touched his mouth to hers. "I believe I can come up with a few ideas," he murmured.

"I like your ideas," Tiffany said a long time later, stretching luxuriously inside the sleeping bag. She was astonishingly warm, considering that Mitch had switched on the heater only a moment ago. She hadn't given him time to do it earlier. Her pent-up emotions had exploded the instant he'd kissed her, and he'd had his hands full persuading her to seek the warmth of the sleeping bag before they were completely naked.

Once they'd zipped themselves into their nylon cocoon, the rest of their clothes had flown in all directions and Tiffany's hands had started moving greedily over his body. She'd wanted to touch him everywhere at once, to feast on his mouth and fill the ache deep inside her with his throbbing heat. For a little while, he was her blanket, her shelter, the touchstone of her existence.

By turns, they had been fierce and tender, frantic and leisurely, overcome by tears and laughter. Reaching a pinnacle higher than ever before, she'd told him again and again of her love, and as their spasms subsided, he'd stroked her hair and whispered the precious words in her ear.

Watching him aim the heater toward them, she smiled. He was a pleasure to look at, strong and fit and breathtakingly virile. As he returned to dive back into the sleeping bag, Tiffany opened her arms to him.

"I'll make you too cold," he said, holding back. "Give me a minute—"

"You have goose bumps," she cut in, wrapping herself around him and gliding her palms over his broad, muscular back. "Besides, it's only fair. You warm me all the time. It's my turn to warm you."

He succumbed and enfolded her in his embrace. "You're doing pretty well," he murmured.

She laughed, already aware of how well. "Come to think of it, I believe it's your turn again." After a little push that rolled them until she was on top, she straddled his lean hips and reached down to guide him into her. "Warm me, Mitch," she whispered. "Warm me the way I love to be warmed."

He bracketed her hips with his two hands and warmed her the way only he could.

By the time they finally got around to the pâtés, cheeses, crusty bread, and cold herbed chicken Mitch had brought out to the tree house on the snowmobile that morning, they were ravenous. They polished it all off as if it were their first meal in weeks.

"Fabulous," Tiffany said, replete at last. Propped up on one elbow as she reclined half in and half out of the sleeping bag, not the least bit cold despite her nudity, she dangled her empty champagne flute between her fingers in an unspoken request for a refill. "You know the great thing about winter picnics?"

"I know several great things about them, especially this one," Mitch said, splashing the pale liquid into her glass. "But what are you referring to in particular?"

She sipped the champagne and tipped back her head, letting the bubbles tickle her tongue and throat for several seconds before answering simply, "No bugs."

Mitch laughed and topped off his own glass. "You know, sweetheart, a woman who can lie around naked in a crude wooden tree house with nothing but an ice-fisherman's heater to protect her against the elements—"

"And a gorgeous hunk of male who keeps her simmering whatever the temperature," she pointed out.

Determinedly, he continued, "A woman who breaks her own ski trail on virgin fields and then climbs a tree to get lunch—"

"It wasn't lunch I was trying to get," Tiffany cut in. "The last time we were up in this tree, we left unfinished business."

He reached across her into the picnic basket, found a chocolate truffle, unwrapped it, and stroked it back and forth over her lips. "Stop interrupting and I'll give you a goody."

She licked at the candy with the tip of her tongue, trying in vain to capture it. "All right," she said after a moment. "But first, give me the truffle."

Shaking his head and laughing, he slipped the chocolate between her lips, then stole some of it in a sweet, creamy kiss.

"What I was trying to say," he went on a few moments later, "was that I won't accept any false modesty from you. You've won our bet hands down. I hereby declare you, once and for all, a True Northerner." He lifted his glass to her in a toast.

Tiffany smiled and accepted his tribute as her due. "A True Northerner," she repeated softly.

"And I owe you a weekend in the Caribbean," he reminded her. "When do you want to collect?"

She turned on her side, her back to him. "I'd forgotten about the bet," she said lightly.

"I hadn't. And I don't intend to welch." He put down his champagne and slid one arm around Tiffany, cupping her breast in his palm. "Think about it, sweetheart." He nibbled teasingly at her earlobe, murmuring, "Picture us basking on a sun-warmed beach, dancing under a tropical moon . . ."

"Tempting," she said on a quick intake of breath, then put down her glass and turned to twine her arms around his neck. "However, lovely as tropical moons and sun-warmed beaches may be, I'm happy here and now. And I've learned from a very wise man that the here and now is all we really have. Let's make it count, Mitch. Let's make every second count for all it's worth."

He hesitated, drawing back his head to search her eyes as if her urgency and her evasiveness had aroused his suspicions, but over the past weeks Tiffany had learned well how to seduce him into forgetfulness.

When the afternoon had stretched into evening, Mitch and Tiffany reluctantly left their hideaway.

The moon that guided them wasn't tropical, but she knew she would never see a more perfect one. Full and pale, drawn in sharp relief against a coal-black sky, it presided over the night like a benevolent empress surveying her domain.

With no wind howling, the swish of the skis was the only sound in the vast stillness. During rest stops, the silence was so complete that Tiffany thought she could hear ice crystals popping in the snow. The air was bracing and sweet, more heady than the champagne she and Mitch had polished off hours ago.

When they reached the house and took off their skis, Mitch drew a deep breath before opening the door to let them inside. "Spring's on the way," he said.

Tiffany smiled up at him. "You can smell it?"

"A little. But mostly I can feel it."

"The rising temperature?"

"No. It has nothing to do with the thermometer. It's something else. A certain softness in the atmosphere. An undercurrent, like an elusive stream of warmth playing around your ankles when you're wading in an icy lake. You think it's there one minute, but the next you're not sure. Right now, it's there. It'll surface fairly soon."

"How long?" Tiffany asked with a trace of wistfulness.

Mitch shrugged. "Hard to tell. That's what makes spring so exciting around here. Or maddening, depending on your outlook."

"Let me guess. For you, it's exciting."

Lowering his head, he brushed his lips over hers. "For me, this will be the most exciting springtime ever."

Tiffany's stomach clenched into a knot. She had to tell him! How would she feel if he were to keep something so important from her?

Yet telling him she wouldn't be with him for the arrival of spring wasn't likely to change anything, except to cast a shadow over their pleasure.

Monday morning would be soon enough.

Monday morning came too quickly.

Sitting across from Mitch at the small table in his kitchen, Tiffany sipped her breakfast coffee and searched for the right way to confess what she'd been holding back since Friday.

She tried telling herself he might take her unexpected departure in stride. After all, this was Mitch she was worrying about. Maybe he'd be relieved that a natural break had come along before things got really heavy.

She didn't believe a bit of it.

Mitch's love for her was real. As real as hers for him. But it was a newborn love, too young and fragile to be tested this way.

"All right, Tiffany, out with it."

Jolted from her inner debate, she looked at Mitch in dismay. She couldn't put off the inevitable any longer.

"Something's been bothering you," he said, leaning forward and folding his arms on the table. "So let's talk. I've been waiting since Friday for you to open up, but you seemed to want us to have our weekend without getting into any serious discussions. The weekend's over now. What's on your mind?"

She swallowed hard, then took a deep breath and blurted out the whole thing. "My company has agreed to everything in the last proposal, but they've decided to send someone else to oversee the transition. They want me back in the Honolulu office by the end of the week. *This* week."

Mitch stared at her, thunderstruck. "Why?"

"I don't know," she said, feeling the blood drain from her face. She hated the way Mitch was looking at her. She'd expected shock. What she saw was anger, barely controlled. "The message didn't go into details. I thought my bosses were pleased with my work, and I told them I'd like to stay on the project, but there's no mistaking the orders."

"You've known since Friday?" Mitch asked, his voice dangerously soft and his eyes boring into hers.

Tiffany nodded and averted her gaze.

He was quiet for a long moment, then said in a monotone, "Okay, you wanted us to enjoy the weekend. And we did, so maybe you made the right decision. But if I hadn't asked, when would you have told me? Or were you planning to tell me at all?"

She looked at him, stung. "Of course I was planning to tell you. This morning, in fact. The only reason you asked before I spoke up was that I had trouble figuring out how to say it."

"And you think *I* don't communicate? You were upset at me for not filling you in on things that happened years ago, and yet you sat on something this important, this . . . this *imminent*?" Unfolding his arms, he slammed his fist down on the table. "Dammit, Tiffany, you claim you love me, and then you present this thing to me as an accomplished fact? What am I supposed to do? Be gracious and say it was nice knowing you, too bad it's over, drop me a postcard from Don Ho's?"

Tears welled up in her eyes. "Mitch, this isn't my decision. I don't want to leave, but I have no choice."

Getting to his feet, Mitch began pacing back and forth across the kitchen, his hands shoved into the pockets of his slacks. "There's always a choice."

"No, there isn't." She grabbed a tissue to wipe her eyes. "You don't tell corporate bosses that you won't go where they want to send you."

He turned to her, lifting one brow. "Why not?"

Tiffany got up and started clearing the table, carrying the dishes to the sink. "Be serious. You know how the world works. My only real options are to do what I'm told or quit my job."

"Quitting your job is out of the question?"

She whirled on him. "To do what? It's not as if I could snap up some other position. I'm not even a citizen here!"

"Stay with me," he said, curving his hands around her shoulders. He studied her for a long moment, then added, "Marry me."

Tiffany couldn't believe her ears. And judging by the look on Mitch's face, he couldn't believe what he'd said. "I don't think you planned that proposal, so I won't hold you to it," she said with an effort, though her heart was clamoring for her to shout a resounding, "Yes!"

"Hold me to it," he urged, pulling her against him. "I want you to hold me to it. You're right. I didn't plan that proposal. I planned a different one. A little more flowery, a lot more romantic, and much better timed." His arms tightened around her. "But the plain, impulsive, stupidly impatient one was every bit as sincere. Marry me, Tiffany. We love each other. What else matters?"

"Nothing else matters," she said, resting her palms against his chest, her cheek on his shoulder. "But everything's happening too quickly. Part of me could do it, Mitch. Part of me has no problem with walking away from my career, my friends, and the only home I've ever known, all to take a gamble on this embryonic love of ours lasting a lifetime. But another part of me isn't quite up to such a giant leap of faith. There'd be such pressure on us, Mitch. We'd feel we had to make things work no matter what, and that's a recipe for failure. Maybe if we could have had more time. . . ." Tipping back her head, she gave him a tentative smile and ventured, "I don't suppose you could take a vacation and go back to Hawaii with me, could you?"

Mitch thought about it for a moment, but finally shook his head. "I could, but under the circumstances I don't think it would solve anything. I'm not the one with doubts, Tiffany. I don't blame you for having them, but I can't make them go away by following you home like some hopeful puppy. This is something you'll have to work out on your own."

"I was afraid you'd say that," Tiffany said. "But the Mitch I'm in love with wouldn't have reacted any other way."

"I'm sorry, sweetheart," he said quietly.

She shook her head. "Don't be. Perhaps we aren't meant to be together. Perhaps fate has thrown this curve at us to keep us from making a mistake."

"Do you honestly believe that?" he asked, stiffening.

Sighing heavily, Tiffany moved out of the shelter of his arms and went to the sink to look out the window at the snow-covered backyard. She'd begun to see the place as a real-life Winter Wonderland, but all of a sudden it just looked cold. "No," she answered in a voice that was barely audible. "But maybe I'd better try to believe it. There's not much else I can do."

THIRTEEN

The scene was like a déjà vu, and Mitch was none too pleased with it.

Once again, he was racing into the airport to meet a passenger arriving from Hawaii. Just like the last time, Pete had come up with some last-minute problem and had asked him to pick up the Paradise Foods representative.

Only this time, that rep wouldn't be Tiffany. He was afraid he'd take one look at her replacement and punch him in the nose.

It occurred to him that he wasn't even sure he was supposed to be meeting a man. Pete had hung up from his call without having given any details. It wasn't a big problem, Mitch thought, not in the mood to give a damn anyway. If necessary, he would have this character paged. But he had the feeling it wouldn't be any harder to spot the second arrival from Hawaii than the first. This one probably had pineapples handpainted on his seersucker shirt.

Checking the arrivals information screen, he saw that the plane had landed. It would be a few more minutes before the passengers showed up at the gate.

Mitch began pacing, trying to stay one step ahead of the memories chasing him, the haunting vision of Tiffany, swinging along in her silly daffodil coat, her blue-black hair curling around her face, her almond eyes looking him over in a way that aroused all his male instincts.

Like the proverbial drowning man, he saw his life passing before his eyes—but only the most important part of his life.

He saw Tiffany's face, lit up with laughter. He saw her struggling along the frozen river, determined to prove she could ski and skate and handle snowshoes as if she'd been born to them. He saw her head drooping and her eyes closing in the middle of one of his long-winded sentences. Her lips parting, welcoming his kiss. Giggling over champagne in the tree house, raving about his inspired picnic, and loving him.

Loving him.

He stopped dead.

The truth crashed in on him. Instead of waiting around, hoping against hope she would come back to him, he should be going after her. He should have left with her in the first place and stayed glued to her side until all her doubts had been put to rest. Jackie had said so, tactfully but firmly. Pete had been more blunt. "You're being a jerk, little brother," he'd exploded the day before. Pete had never been one for sugar-coating. "Why aren't you in Honolulu? What did you expect from Tiffany? The woman knows you for a couple of months. You're tight-lipped about yourself for most of that time, stubbornly letting her think you're some kind of flake and an incurable Don Juan to boot, and when you announce that you love her and want to marry her, she's supposed to trust you enough to put everything in her own life on the line? How you could have put her on that plane and let her go is beyond me. You, of all people. The guy who goes after what he wants and gets it come hell or high water."

Mitch felt a wave of sickness pass over him. Suddenly he saw what he'd done. It was a strange, horrible replay of the past. When he should have bided his time, laying the groundwork and making certain the moment was right to shoot for the biggest prize of all, he'd turned hotshot. Only this time the prize he'd lost wasn't Olympic gold. This time he'd lost Tiffany.

How could he have been so stupid? Why had he believed that a few words from him, a few romantic trysts, a few hours of passion, would give Tiffany all the reassurance she needed?

Why had he lost patience at the very moment when he'd needed it most?

He made up his mind. "Honolulu, here I come," he muttered as he saw the first trickle of passengers coming through the gate. He would deliver this interloper to Pete at the packaging plant. He'd even try to be gracious, for the sake of the deal Tiffany had been so proud of.

And then he would go home to pack and book the next flight to the South Pacific.

Eager to get moving, he wished he'd made a sign he could hold up that would say who he was and which passenger he was there to meet. It might have speeded things up.

Suddenly he caught a glimpse of something that made his heart leap to his throat. Yellow. Daffodil-yellow. Hem swinging, lifting, revealing long, shapely, slender legs.

He was sure he was hallucinating. He wanted Tiffany so much, he was seeing her when she wasn't there.

But if she was a dream, she was a vivid one. Smiling, eyes shining, she saw him and started walking faster.

"Tiffany," he whispered.

She broke into a run.

"Tiffany!" He bolted forward. It was time to meet her halfway. More than halfway if he could get there fast enough. He ran the slalom of his life past the bodies in his path, reaching her in a race that shattered all records. "Tiffany," he said again as he hauled her into his arms. "Oh baby, sweetheart, love . . ." There weren't enough endearments. There was no way to express the joy flooding through him. He sought her mouth and convinced himself she was real by tasting her sweetness and losing himself in her soft warmth.

Tiffany felt as if the airport was spinning. She didn't care. Mitch was holding her. The whole planet could whirl off into another galaxy, and she would feel safe and at home as long as she was in his arms.

When he finally released her mouth, he laced his fingers through her hair and pressed her cheek to his chest, his other arm so tight around her, she knew he was never going to let her go again. "You came back," he said, rubbing his face against her hair. "You came back to me."

"I had to," she murmured. Tipping back her head to smile up at him through happy tears, she said, "I was freezing to death in Hawaii. There's only one place in the world where I can be warm. With you, Mitch. Only with you."

He gazed down at her, his own eyes moist. "I'd have been there by tomorrow to warm you, sweetheart. It took me a while, but I finally wised up. Now, do you want to stay here, or should we buy two tickets and go straight back to Honolulu?"

"I want to stay. I *have* to stay. I have a job to do here."

"A job? You're the rep I'm here to meet?"

She nodded. "I'd decided to quit and fly back here to you, but I kept remembering how you said there were other options. I thought about the way you'd battled your way back from total disaster ten years ago, and I figured I could at least fight for my job. So I screwed up my courage, asked for a meeting with the company brass, and told them that the Winnipeg project had been mine from the start and ought to remain mine. And it worked! The craziest part is that they'd thought they were doing me a favor by sending in someone who was more accustomed to cold weather. They wanted to *reward* me! Can you imagine?"

"They must be idiots, thinking you'd want to stay in a tropical Eden when you can have all this," he said thickly, waving a hand toward the windows that looked out on brown, muddy ground dotted with great patches of dirty snow.

Tiffany smiled, her gaze remaining on Mitch. "They must be."

A thought occurred to Mitch. It wasn't too troubling, given what Tiffany had already told him, but he had to ask. "What happens when your liaison work is finished?"

"Maybe it won't be finished. I have some ideas about setting up a Winnipeg office to keep a closer eye on several mainland operations, what with this location being pretty much smack in the middle of the continent. But if that plan doesn't work out, I don't care. I'm in love with a wonderful rogue, and that's the bottom line." She hesitated, then added softly, "Whatever happens to me careerwise, does that impulsive proposal of yours still stand?"

Mitch felt as if he could breathe again for the first time in a long while. "It wasn't an impulsive proposal, sweetheart. Back in February I said I was going for the gold with you, and even then I was talking about gold wedding bands. Yes, it still stands, but I'll ask again, just for the record. Will you marry me, Tiffany?"

"Oh Mitch," she whispered. "Oh yes, Mitch, yes."

He closed his eyes and struggled to absorb what seemed like a miracle. When he opened them again, he tightened his arms around Tiffany. "God, I love you," he murmured.

In the next second, Tiffany saw his features take on the purposeful expression that meant he was already making decisions. "A June wedding at the farm would be nice. And the honeymoon has to be in the Caribbean, of course . . ."

"Mitch," Tiffany said, putting a finger to his lips.

He raised his brows questioningly.

"You're being bossy again."

Rolling his eyes, he laughed and released her, draping one arm around her shoulders as they walked over to the baggage carousel. "Okay, you're in charge. How do you want to do it?"

She thought about the matter for a few seconds, then lifted her chin. "A June wedding at the farm would be nice. And you do owe me a trip to the Caribbean. . . ."

Mitch tipped back his head and exploded in a laugh of sheer, exuberant joy. "From now on, sweetheart, I promise to defer to your wishes in all matters."

"And I'll never argue with you about anything again," she vowed with mock gravity.

He laughed again and gave her a quick hug, then

spotted her luggage and pulled it off the conveyor belt. "And if either of us believes what the other said, the Manitoba Winter-Blooming Snowflower will carpet the streets of Winnipeg every day of the year for the rest of our natural lives."

Tiffany never doubted for a moment that it would.

THE EDITOR'S CORNER

The heroines in September's LOVESWEPT novels have a secret dream of love and passion—and they find the answer to their wishes with FANTASY MEN! Whether he's a dangerous rogue, a dashing prince, or a lord of the jungle, he's a masterful hero who knows just the right moves that dazzle the senses, the teasing words that stoke white-hot desire, and the seductive caresses that promise ecstasy. He's the kind of man who can make a woman do anything, the only man who can fulfill her deepest longing. And the heroines find they'll risk all, even their hearts, to make their dreams come true with FANTASY MEN. . . .

Our first dream lover sizzles off the pages of Sandra Chastain's **THE MORNING AFTER**, LOVESWEPT #636. Razor Cody had come to Savannah seeking revenge on the man who'd destroyed his business, but instead he found a fairy-tale princess whose violet eyes and spun-gold hair made him yearn for what he'd never dared to hope would be his! Rachel Kimble told him she'd known he was coming and hinted of the treasure he'd find if he stayed, but she couldn't conceal her shocking desire for the mysterious stranger! Vowing to keep her safe from shadows that haunted her nights, Razor fought to heal Rachel's pain, as her gentle touch soothed his own. **THE MORNING AFTER** is Sandra Chastain at her finest.

Cindy Gerard invites you to take one last summer swim with her fantasy man in **DREAM TIDE**, LOVESWEPT #637. Patrick Ryan was heart-stoppingly gorgeous—all temptation and trouble in a pair of jeans. And Merry Clare Thomas was stunned to wake up in his arms . . . and in his bed! She'd taken refuge in her rental cottage, never expecting the tenant to return that night—or that he'd look exactly like the handsome wanderer of a hundred years ago who'd been making steamy love to her in her dreams every night for a week. Was it destiny or just coincidence that Pat called her his flame, his firebrand, just as her dream lover had? Overwhelmed by need, dazzled by passion, Merry responded with fierce pleasure to Pat's wildfire caresses, possessed by him in a magical enchantment that just couldn't be real. But Cindy's special touch is all too real in this tale of a fantasy come true.

TROUBLE IN PARADISE, LOVESWEPT #638, is another winner from one of LOVESWEPT's rising stars, Susan Connell. Just lying in a hammock, Reilly Anderson awakened desire potent enough to take her breath away, but Allison Richards fought her attraction to the bare-chested hunk who looked like he'd stepped out of an adventure movie! Gazing at the long-legged vision who insisted that he help her locate her missing brother-in-law, Reilly knew that trouble had arrived . . . the kind of trouble a man just had to taste! Reilly drew her into a paradise of pleasure, freeing her spirit with tender savagery and becoming her very own Tarzan, Lord of the Jungle. He swore he'd make her see she had filled his heart with joy and that he'd never let her go.

Linda Jenkins's fantasy is a **SECRET ADMIRER,** LOVESWEPT #639. An irresistible rascal, Jack was the golden prince of her secret girlhood fantasies, but Kary Lucas knew Jack Rowland could never be hers! Back then he'd always teased her about being the smartest girl in town—how could she believe the charming nomad with the bad-boy grin when he insisted he was home to stay at last? Jack infuriated her and made her ache with sensual longing. But when mysterious gifts began arriving, presents and notes that seemed to know her private passions, Kary was torn: tempted by the romance of her unknown knight, yet thrilled by the explosive heat of Jack's embraces, the insatiable need he aroused. Linda's fantasy man has just the right combination of dreamy mystery and thrilling reality to keep your nights on fire!

Terry Lawrence works her own unique LOVESWEPT magic with **DANCING ON THE EDGE,** LOVE-SWEPT #640. Stunt coordinator Greg Ford needed a woman to stand up to him, to shake him up, and Annie Oakley Cartwright decided she was just the brazen daredevil to do it! Something burned between them from the moment they met, made Annie want to rise to his challenge, to tempt the man who made her lips tingle just by looking. Annie trusted him with her body, ached to ease his sorrow with her rebel's heart. Once she'd reminded him life was a series of gambles, and love the biggest one of all, she could only hope he would dance with his spitfire as long as their music played. Terry's spectacular romance will send you looking for your own stuntman!

Leanne Banks has a regal fantasy man for you in **HIS ROYAL PLEASURE,** LOVESWEPT #641. Prince Alex swept into her peaceful life like a swashbuckling pirate, confidently expecting Katherine Kendall to let him spend a month at her island camp—never confessing the secret of his birth to the sweet and tender lady who made him want to break all the rules! He made her feel beautiful, made her dream of dancing in the dark and succumbing to forbidden kisses under a moonlit sky. Katherine wondered who he was, but Alex was an expert when it came to games lovers play, and he made her moan with ecstasy at his sizzling touch . . . until she learned his shocking secret. Leanne is at her steamy best with this sexy fantasy man.

Happy reading!

With warmest wishes,

Nita Taublib

Nita Taublib

Associate Publisher

P.S. On the next pages is a preview of the Bantam titles on sale *now* at your favorite bookstore.

Don't miss these exciting books by your
favorite Bantam authors

On sale in July:
FANTA C
by Sandra Brown

CRY WOLF
by Tami Hoag

*TWICE IN A
LIFETIME*
by Christy Cohen

THE TESTIMONY
by Sharon and Tom Curtis

And in hardcover from Doubleday
STRANGER IN MY ARMS
by R. J. Kaiser

From *New York Times*
Bestselling Author

Sandra Brown

Fanta C

The bestselling author of Temperatures Rising *and*
French Silk, *Sandra Brown has created a sensation with her
contemporary novels. Now, in this classic novel she offers a
tender, funny, and deeply sensual story about a woman
caught between the needs of her children, her career, and her
own passionate heart.*

Elizabeth Burke's days are filled with the business of
running an elegant boutique and caring for her two
small children. But her nights are long and empty
since the death of her husband two years before,
and she spends them dreaming of the love and romance
that might have been. Then Thad Randolph steps
into her life—a man right out of her most intimate
fantasies.

Elizabeth doesn't believe in fairy tales, and she knows
all too well that happy endings happen only in books.
Now she wishes she could convince herself that friend-

ship is all she wants from Thad. But the day will come when she'll finally have to make a choice—to remain forever true to her memories or to let go of the past and risk loving once more.

Cry Wolf
by
Tami Hoag

author of *Still Waters* and *Lucky's Lady*

Tami Hoag is one of today's premier writers of romantic suspense. Publisher's Weekly *calls her "a master of the genre" for her powerful combination of gripping suspense and sizzling passion. Now from the incredibly talented author of Sarah's Sin, Lucky's Lady, and Still Waters comes* Cry Wolf, *her most dangerously thrilling novel yet. . . .*

All attorney Laurel Chandler wanted was a place to hide, to escape the painful memories of a case that had destroyed her career, her marriage, and nearly her life. But coming home to the peaceful, tree-lined streets of her old hometown won't give Laurel the serenity she craves. For in the sultry heat of a Louisiana summer, she'll find herself pursued by Jack Boudreaux, a gorgeous stranger whose carefree smile hides a private torment . . . and by a murderer who enjoys the hunt as much as the kill.

In the following scene, Laurel is outside of Frenchie's, a local hangout, when she realizes she's unable to drive the car she borrowed. When Jack offers to drive her home, she has no alternative but to accept.

"Women shouldn't accept rides from men they barely know," she said, easing herself down in the bucket seat, her gaze fixed on Jack.

"What?" he asked, splaying a hand across his bare chest, the picture of hurt innocence. "You think *I'm* the Bayou Strangler? Oh, man . . ."

"You could be the man."

"What makes you think it's a man? Could be a woman."

"Could be, but not likely. Serial killers tend to be white males in their thirties."

He grinned wickedly, eyes dancing. "Well, I fit that bill, I guess, but I don't have to kill ladies to get what I want, angel."

He leaned into her space, one hand sliding across the back of her seat, the other edging along the dash, corralling her. Laurel's heart kicked into overdrive as he came closer, though fear was not the dominant emotion. It should have been, but it wasn't.

That strange sense of desire and anticipation crept along her nerves. If she leaned forward, he would kiss her. She could see the promise in his eyes and felt something wild and reckless and completely foreign to her rise up in answer, pushing her to close the distance, to take the chance. His eyes dared her, his mouth lured—masculine, sexy, lips slightly parted in invitation. What fear she felt was of herself, of this attraction she didn't want.

"It's power, not passion," she whispered, barely able to find her voice at all.

Jack blinked. The spell was broken. "What?"

"They kill for power. Exerting power over other human beings gives them a sense of omnipotence . . . among other things."

He sat back and fired the 'Vette's engine, his brows drawn as he contemplated what she'd said. "So, why are you going with me?"

"Because there are a dozen witnesses standing on the gallery who saw me get in the car with you. You'd be the last person seen with me alive, which would automatically make you a suspect. Patrons in the bar will testify that I spurned your advances. That's motive. If you were the killer, you'd be pretty stupid to take me away from here and kill me, and if this killer was stupid, someone would have caught him by now."

He scowled as he put the car in gear. "And here I thought you'd say it was my charm and good looks."

"Charming men don't impress me," she said flatly, buckling her seat belt.

Then what does? Jack wondered as he guided the car slowly out of the parking lot. A sharp mind, a man of principles? He had one, but wasn't the other. Not that it mattered. He wasn't interested in Laurel Chandler. She would be too much trouble. And she was too uptight to go for a man who spent most of his waking hours at Frenchie's—unlike her sister, who went for any man who could get it up. Night and day, those two. He couldn't help wondering why.

The Chandler sisters had been raised to be belles. Too good for the likes of him, ol' Blackie would have said. Too good for a no-good coonass piece of trash. He glanced across at Laurel, who sat with her hands folded and her glasses perched on her slim little nose and thought the old man would have been right. She was prim and proper, Miss Law and Order, full of morals and high ideals and upstanding qualities . . . and fire . . . and pain . . . and secrets in her eyes. . . .

"Was I to gather from that conversation with T-Grace that you used to be an attorney?" she asked as they turned onto Dumas and headed back toward downtown.

He smiled, though it held no real amusement, only cynicism. "Sugar, 'attorney' is too polite a word for what I used to be. I was a corporate shark for Tristar Chemical."

Laurel tried to reconcile the traditional three-piece-suit corporate image with the man who sat across from her, a baseball cap jammed down backward on his head, his Hawaiian shirt hanging open to reveal the hard, tanned body of a light heavyweight boxer. "What happened?"

What happened? A simple question as loaded as a shotgun that had been primed and pumped. What happened? He had succeeded. He had set out to prove to his old man that he could do something, be something, make big money. It hadn't mattered that Blackie was long dead and gone to hell.

The old man's ghost had driven him. He had succeeded, and in the end he had lost everything.

"I turned on 'em," he said, skipping the heart of the story. The pain he endured still on Evie's behalf was his own private hell. He didn't share it with anyone. "*Rogue Lawyer*. I think they're gonna make it into a TV movie one of these days."

"What do you mean, you turned on them?"

"I mean, I unraveled the knots I'd tied for them in the paper trail that divorced them from the highly illegal activities of shipping and dumping hazardous waste," he explained, not entirely sure why he was telling her. Most of the time when people asked, he just blew it off, made a joke, and changed the subject. "The Feds took a dim view of the company. The company gave me the ax, and the Bar Association kicked my ass out."

"You were disbarred for revealing illegal, potentially dangerous activities to the federal government?" Laurel said, incredulous. "But that's—"

"The way it is, sweetheart," he growled, slowing the 'Vette as the one and only stop light in Bayou Breaux turned red. He rested his hand on the stick shift and gave Laurel a hard look. "Don' make me out to be a hero, sugar. I'm nobody's saint. I lost it," he said bitterly. "I crashed and burned. I went down in a ball of flame, and I took the company with me. I had my reasons, and none of them had anything to do with such noble causes as the protection of the environment."

"But—"

"'But,' you're thinking now, 'mebbe this Jack, he isn't such a bad guy after all,' yes?" His look turned sly, speculative. He chuckled as she frowned. She didn't want to think he could read her so easily. If they'd been playing poker, he would have cleaned out her pockets.

"Well, you're wrong, angel," he murmured darkly, his mouth twisting with bitter amusement as her blue eyes widened. "I'm as bad as they come." Then he flashed his famous grin, dimples biting into his cheeks. "But I'm a helluva good time."

Twice in a Lifetime
by
Christy Cohen

author of *Private Scandals*

***Fifteen years ago, an act of betrayal tore
four best friends apart . . .***

SARAH. *A lonely newlywed in a new town, she was thrilled
when Annabel came into her life. Suddenly Sarah had
someone to talk to and the best part was that her husband
seemed to like Annabel too.*

JESSE. *With his sexy good looks and dangerous aura, he
could have had any woman. But he'd chosen sweet, innocent
Sarah, who touched not only his body but his soul. So why
couldn't Jesse stop dreaming of his wife's best friend?*

ANNABEL. *Beautiful, desirable, and enigmatic, she
yearned for something more exciting than being a wife and
mother. And nothing was more exciting than making a man
like Jesse want her.*

PATRICK. *Strong and tender, this brilliant scientist
learned that the only way to keep Annabel his wife was to
turn a blind eye—until the day came when he couldn't
pretend anymore.*

In the following scene, Jesse and Annabel feel trapped at a birthday party that Sarah is hosting and they have to escape into the surrounding neighborhood.

As they walked through the neighborhood of newer homes, Jesse's arm was around her. He could feel every curve of her. Her breast was pressed against his chest. Her leg brushed his as she walked.

"Sarah's probably pissed," he said.

Annabel laughed. "She'll get over it. Besides, Patrick the knight will save her."

Jesse looked at her.

"Have you noticed they've been talking to each other a lot?"

"Of course. Patrick calls her from work. And sometimes at night. He's too honest not to tell me."

When Annabel pressed herself closer to Jesse, he lowered his hand a little on her shoulder. An inch or two farther down and he would be able to touch the silky skin of her breast.

"Do you love him?" he asked.

Annabel stopped suddenly and Jesse dropped his hand. She turned to stare at him.

"What do you think?"

With her eyes challenging him, Jesse took a step closer.

"I think you don't give a fuck about him. Maybe you did when you married him, but it didn't last long. Now it's me you're after."

Annabel tossed back her black hair, laughing.

"God, what an ego. You think a little harmless flirting means I'm hot for you. No wonder Sarah needed a change of pace."

Jesse grabbed her face in one hand and squeezed. He watched tears come to her eyes as he increased the pressure on her jaw, but she didn't cry out.

"Sarah did not cheat on me," he said. "You got the story wrong."

He pushed her away and started walking back toward the house. Annabel took a deep breath, then came after him.

"What Sarah did or didn't do isn't the point," she said when she reached him. "She's not the one who's unhappy."

Jesse glanced at her, but kept walking.

"You're saying I am?"

"It's obvious, Jesse. Little Miss Perfect Sarah isn't all that exciting. Especially for a man like you. I'll bet that's why you have to ride your Harley all the time. To replace all the passion you gave up when you married her."

Jesse looked up over the houses, to Mt. Rainier in the distance.

"I sold the bike," he said. "Two weeks ago."

"My God, why?"

Jesse stopped again.

"Because Sarah asked me to. And because, no matter what you think, I love her."

They stared at each other for a long time. The wind was cool and Jesse watched gooseflesh prickle Annabel's skin. He didn't know whom he was trying to convince more, Annabel or himself.

"I think we should go back," Jesse said.

Annabel nodded. "Of course. You certainly don't want to make little Sarah mad. You've got to be the dutiful husband. If Sarah says sell your bike, you sell your bike. If she wants you to entertain twelve kids like a clown, then you do it. If—"

Jesse grabbed her, only intending to shut her up. But when he looked down at her, he knew she had won. She had been whittling away at him from the very beginning. She had made him doubt himself, and Sarah, and everything he thought he should be. He grabbed her hair and tilted her head back. She slid her hands up around his neck. Her fingers were cool and silky.

Later, he would look back and try to convince himself that she was the one who initiated the kiss, that she pulled his head down and pressed her red lips to his. Maybe she initiated it, maybe he did. All he knew was that he was finally touching her, kissing her, his tongue was in her mouth and it felt better than he'd ever imagined.

The Testimony

A classic romance by

Sharon & Tom Curtis

bestselling authors of *The Golden Touch*

It had been so easy falling in love with Jesse Ludan . . . with his ready smile and laughing green eyes, his sensual body and clever journalist's mind. The day Christine became his wife was the happiest day of her life. But for the past six months, Jesse's idealism has kept him in prison. And now he's coming home a hero . . . and a stranger.

In the following scene Jesse and Christine are alone in the toolshed behind her house only hours after Jesse's return . . .

"Jess?" Her blue eyes had grown solemn.

"What, love?"

"I don't know how to ask this . . . Jesse, I don't want to blast things out of you that you're not ready to talk about but I have to know . . ." An uncertain pause. "How much haven't you told me? Was prison . . . was it horrible?"

Was it horrible? she had asked him. There she stood in her silk knit sweater, her Gucci shoes, and one of the expensive skirts she wore that clung, but never too tightly, to her slender thighs, asking him if prison was horrible. Her eyes were serious and bright with the fetching sincerity that seemed like such a poor defense against the darker aspects of life and that, paradoxically, always made him want to bare his soul to that uncallused sanity. The soft taut skin over her nose and cheeks shone slightly in the highly filtered light, paling her freckles, giving a fragility to her face with its combined suggestion of sturdiness and sensitivity. He would have thought four years of marriage might have banished any unease he felt about what a sociologist would label the "class difference" of their backgrounds, yet looking at her now, he had never felt it more strongly.

There was a reel of fishing line in his right hand. Where had it come from? The window shelf. He let her thick curl slide from his fingers and walked slowly to the shelf, reaching up to replace the roll, letting the motion hide his face while he spoke.

"It was a little horrible." He leaned his back against the workbench, gripping the edge. Gently shifting the focus away from himself, he said, "Was it a little horrible here without me?"

"It was a lot horrible here without you." The admission seemed to relieve some of her tension. "Not that I'm proud of being so dependent on a man, mind you."

"Say three Our Fathers, two Hail Marys, and read six months of back issues of *Ms*. magazine. Go in peace, Daughter, and sin no more." He gestured a blessing. Then, putting a palm lightly over his own heart, he added, "I had the same thing. Desolation."

"You missed the daily dose of me?"

"I missed the daily dose of you."

Her toes turned inward, freckled fingers threaded anxiously together. The round chin dropped and she gazed at him from under her lashes, a mime of bashfulness.

"So here we are—alone at last," she breathed.

Sometimes mime was a game for Christine, sometimes a refuge. In college she had joined a small troupe that passed a hat in the city parks. To combat her shyness, she still used it, retreating as though to the anonymity of whiteface and costume.

He could feel the anxiety pent up in her. *Show me you're all right, Jesse.* Something elemental in his life seemed to hinge on his comforting her. He searched desperately for the self he had been before prison, trying to clone the person she would know and recognize and feel safe with.

"Alone, and in such romantic surroundings," he said, taking a step toward her. His heel touched a shovel blade, sending a shiver of reaction through the nervously perched lawn implements that lined the wall. Some interesting quirk of physics kept them upright except for one rake that came whacking to the floor at his feet. "Ah, the hazards of these secret liaisons! We've got to stop meeting like this—the gardener is beginning to suspect."

"The gardener I can handle, but when a man in his prime is nearly cut down by a rake . . ."

"A *dangerous* rake." His voice lowered. "This, my dear, is Milwaukee's most notorious rake. More women have surrendered their virtue to him than to the legions of Caesar." He lifted the rake tines upward and made it walk toward her, giving it a lascivious whisper. "Don't fight it, *cara.* Your body was made for love. With me you can experience the fullness of your womanhood."

She laughed at his notion of the things rakes say, garnered three years ago from a teasing thumb-through of a certain deliciously fat romance novel that she had meant to keep better hidden. Raising one hand dramatically to ward off the rake, she said, "Leaf me alone, lecher!"

The rake took an offended dip and marched back to the wall in a huff. "Reject me if you must," it said in a wounded tone, "but must I endure a bad pun about my honorable profession? I thought women were supposed to love a rake," it added hopefully.

A smile hovered near the edge of her husband's mobile lips. Christine recognized a certain quality in it that made her heart beat harder. As his hands came lightly down on her shoulders, her lips parted without her will and her gaze traveled up to meet the shadow play of desire in his eyes.

"Some women prefer their very own husbands." There was a slight breathless quiver in her voice, and the throb of tightening pressure in her lungs.

"Hot damn. A compliment." Jesse let his thumbs slide down the front of her shoulders, rotating them with gentle sensuality over the soft flesh that lay above the rise of her breasts. She had begun to tremble under the sure movements of his fingers, and her slipping control brought back to him all the warm nights they had shared, the tangled sheets, the pungent musky air. He remembered the rosy flush of her upraised nipples and the way they felt on his lips. . . .

It had been so long, more than six months, since they had been together, six months since he had even seen a woman. He wondered if she realized that, or guessed how her nearness made his senses skyrocket. He wanted her to give up her body to him, to offer herself to him like an expanding breath for him to touch and taste and fill, to watch her bluebell eyes grow smoky with rapture. But though he drew her close so that he could feel the lovely fullness of her small breasts pressing into his ribs, he made no move to lower his hands or to take her lips. She seemed entrancingly clean, like a just-bathed child, and as pure. The damaged part of him came to her almost as a supplicant, unwhole before her wholesomeness. Can I touch you, love? Tell me it's all right . . .

She couldn't have heard his thoughts, or seen them, because he had learned too well to disguise them; yet her hands came to him like an answer, her fingers entwined behind his neck, pulling him toward her warm mouth. He took a breath as her lips skimmed over his and another much harder one as she stood on her toes to heighten the contact. Her tongue probed shyly at his lips and then forced an entrance, her body twisting slowly into his, a sinuous shock against his thighs.

He murmured something, random words of desire he couldn't remember as he said them; the pressure of her lips increased, and he felt thought begin to leave, and a growing pressure behind his eyelids. His hands were drifting over her blindly, as in a vision, until a shuddering fever ran through his veins and he dragged her close, pulling her hard into him, holding her there with one arm while the other slid under her sweater, his fingers spreading over the powdery softness of her skin. A surprised moan swept from her mouth into his lips as his hand lightly covered her breast. His palm absorbed her warmth, her delicate shape, and the thrillingly uneven pattern of her respiration before slipping to the fine heat and velvet distension of her nipple.

This time he heard his own whisper, telling her that he loved her, that she bewitched him, and then repeating her name again and again with the rhythm of his mouth and tongue. He was overcome, lost in her elemental femaleness, his pulse hammering through his body. Leaning her back, bringing his mouth hard against hers, he poured his kiss into her until their rapid breathing came together and he could feel every silken inch of her with the front of his body.

A keen breeze rattled the roof of the shed. It might have been the sound that brought him back, or perhaps some inner thermostat of his own, but he became aware suddenly that he was going to take her here in old man Jaroch's toolshed. And then he thought, Oh, Christ, how hard have I been holding her? His own muscles ached from the force, and he brought his head up to examine her upturned face. Sleepy lashes dusted her cheeks. A contented smile curved over damp and swollen lips. Her skin was lustrous. He pulled her into the curve of his arm with a relieved sigh, cradling her while he tried to contain his overwhelming appetite. Not here, Ludan. Not like this, with half your mind on freeze.

Kissing her once on each eyelid, he steeled his self-restraint and put her very gently from him. Her eyes flew open; her gaze leaped curiously to his.

"Heart of my heart, I'm sorry," he said softly, smiling at her, "but if I don't take my shameless hands off you . . ."

"I might end up experiencing the fullness of my woman-hood in a toolshed?" she finished for him. Her returning grin had a sexy sweetness that tested his resolution. "It's not the worst idea I've ever heard."

But it is, Chris, he thought. Because enough of me hasn't walked out of that cell yet to make what would happen between us into an act of love. And the trust I see in your eyes would never allow me to give you less.

OFFICIAL RULES

To enter the sweepstakes below carefully follow all instructions found elsewhere in this offer.

The **Winners Classic** will award prizes with the following approximate maximum values: 1 Grand Prize: $26,500 (or $25,000 cash alternate); 1 First Prize: $3,000; 5 Second Prizes: $400 each; 35 Third Prizes: $100 each; 1,000 Fourth Prizes: $7.50 each. Total maximum retail value of Winners Classic Sweepstakes is $42,500. Some presentations of this sweepstakes may contain individual entry numbers corresponding to one or more of the aforementioned prize levels. To determine the Winners, individual entry numbers will first be compared with the winning numbers preselected by computer. For winning numbers not returned, prizes will be awarded in random drawings from among all eligible entries received. Prize choices may be offered at various levels. If a winner chooses an automobile prize, all license and registration fees, taxes, destination charges and, other expenses not offered herein are the responsibility of the winner. If a winner chooses a trip, travel must be complete within one year from the time the prize is awarded. Minors must be accompanied by an adult. Travel companion(s) must also sign release of liability. Trips are subject to space and departure availability. Certain black-out dates may apply.

The following applies to the sweepstakes named above:

No purchase necessary. You can also enter the sweepstakes by sending your name and address to: P.O. Box 508, Gibbstown, N.J. 08027. Mail each entry separately. Sweepstakes begins 6/1/93. Entries must be received by 12/30/94. Not responsible for lost, late, damaged, misdirected, illegible or postage due mail. Mechanically reproduced entries are not eligible. All entries become property of the sponsor and will not be returned.

Prize Selection/Validations: Selection of winners will be conducted no later than 5:00 PM on January 28, 1995, by an independent judging organization whose decisions are final. Random drawings will be held at 1211 Avenue of the Americas, New York, N.Y. 10036. Entrants need not be present to win. Odds of winning are determined by total number of entries received. Circulation of this sweepstakes is estimated not to exceed 200 million. All prizes are guaranteed to be awarded and delivered to winners. Winners will be notified by mail and may be required to complete an affidavit of eligibility and release of liability which must be returned within 14 days of date on notification or alternate winners will be selected in a random drawing. Any prize notification letter or any prize returned to a participating sponsor, Bantam Doubleday Dell Publishing Group, Inc., its participating divisions or subsidiaries, or the independent judging organization as undeliverable will be awarded to an alternate winner. Prizes are not transferable. No substitution for prizes except as offered or as may be necessary due to unavailability, in which case a prize of equal or greater value will be awarded. Prizes will be awarded approximately 90 days after the drawing. All taxes are the sole responsibility of the winners. Entry constitutes permission (except where prohibited by law) to use winners' names, hometowns, and likenesses for publicity purposes without further or other compensation. Prizes won by minors will be awarded in the name of parent or legal guardian.

Participation: Sweepstakes open to residents of the United States and Canada, except for the province of Quebec. Sweepstakes sponsored by Bantam Doubleday Dell Publishing Group, Inc., (BDD), 1540 Broadway, New York, NY 10036. Versions of this sweepstakes with different graphics and prize choices will be offered in conjunction with various solicitations or promotions by different subsidiaries and divisions of BDD. Where applicable, winners will have their choice of any prize offered at level won. Employees of BDD, its divisions, subsidiaries, advertising agencies, independent judging organization, and their immediate family members are not eligible.

Canadian residents, in order to win, must first correctly answer a time limited arithmetical skill testing question. Void in Puerto Rico, Quebec and wherever prohibited or restricted by law. Subject to all federal, state, local and provincial laws and regulations. For a list of major prize winners (available after 1/29/95): send a self-addressed, stamped envelope entirely separate from your entry to: Sweepstakes Winners, P.O. Box 517, Gibbstown, NJ 08027. Requests must be received by 12/30/94. DO NOT SEND ANY OTHER CORRESPONDENCE TO THIS P.O. BOX.

Don't miss these fabulous Bantam women's fiction titles on sale in July

CRY WOLF

56160-X $5.50/6.50 in Canada

by **Tami Hoag**

Author of STILL WATERS

A juicy novel of romantic suspense set in the steamy Louisiana Bayou by the author Publishers Weekly *calls "a master of the genre."*

FANTA C

56274-6 $5.99/6.99 in Canada

by **Sandra Brown**

Author of TEMPERATURES RISING

A single mother struggles to balance the needs of work, home, and the passionate desires of her own heart.

TWICE IN A LIFETIME

56298-3 $4.99/5.99 in Canada

by **Christy Cohen**

Author of PRIVATE SCANDALS

A gripping story of two women who find their friendship threatened when they each fall in love with the other's husband.

THE TESTIMONY

29948-4 $4.50/5.50 in Canada

by **Sharon and Tom Curtis**

Authors of SUNSHINE AND SHADOW

"[THE TESTIMONY] is one of the finest books I've ever read." —Romantic Times.

Don't miss these fabulous Bantam women's fiction titles On sale in August

• THE MAGNIFICENT ROGUE
by Iris Johansen, author of THE TIGER PRINCE

From the glittering court of Queen Elizabeth to the craggy cliffs of a Scottish island, THE MAGNIFICENT ROGUE weaves a passionate tale of two lovers who must risk their lives to defy the ultimate treachery. ____29944-1 $5.99/6.99 in Canada

• VIRTUE
by Jane Feather, author of THE EAGLE AND THE DOVE

"An instantaneous attention-grabber....Well crafted...with a strong compelling story and utterly delightful characters."
—*Romantic Times* ____56054-9 $4.99/5.99 in Canada

• BENEATH A SAPPHIRE SEA
by Jessica Bryan, author of ACROSS A WINE-DARK SEA

The passionate tale of a beautiful scholar who encounters a race of rare and wondrous men and women under the sea who face a grave peril. ____56221-5 $4.99/5.99 in Canada

• TEMPTING EDEN
by Maureen Reynolds, author of SMOKE EYES

The passion between a beautiful aristocrat and a famous private invistigator nearly kills them both when they pursue her missing twin. ____56435-8 $4.99/5.99 in Canada

Ask for these books at your local bookstore or use this page to order.